RnXS

SS
2024

You know you want to read
ALL the Pizza and Taco books!

WHO'S THE BEST?

BEST PARTY EVER!

SUPER-AWESOME COMIC!

TOO COOL FOR SCHOOL

ROCK OUT!

DARE TO BE SCARED!

WRESTLING MANIA!

BEST CHRISTMAS EVER!
(COMING IN SEPTEMBER 2024)

Pizza and Taco

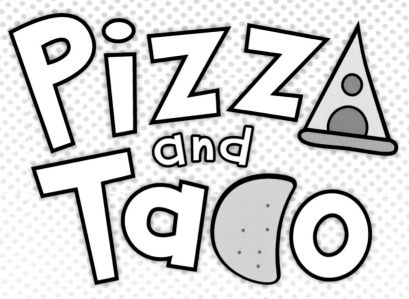

WRESTLING MANIA!

STEPHEN SHASKAN

Who's your favorite wrestler?

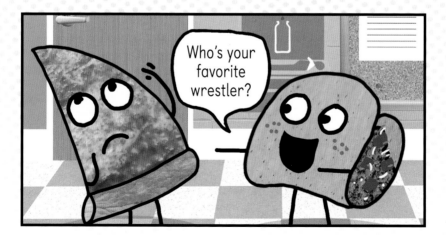

A STEPPING STONE BOOK™
Random House New York

To Collin, Claire, Ruby, and Henry

Visit us on the Web! rhcbooks.com

Educators and librarians, for a variety of teaching tools, visit us at RHTeachersLibrarians.com

Library of Congress Cataloging-in-Publication Data
Name: Shaskan, Stephen, author.
Title: Pizza and Taco: wrestling mania! / Stephen Shaskan.
Other titles: Wrestling mania!
Description: First edition. | New York: Random House Children's Books, [2024] | Series: Pizza and Taco; book 7 | "A Stepping Stone book" | Audience: Ages 5–8 | Summary: "Pizza's and Taco's moms want them to join a sports team, so when they see the wrestling sign-up sheet at school they choose their wrestling names and create signature moves, hoping to join the club." —Provided by publisher.
Identifiers: LCCN 2022059867 (print) | LCCN 2022059868 (ebook) | ISBN 978-0-593-70346-5 (trade) | ISBN 978-0-593-70347-2 (lib. bdg.) | ISBN 978-0-593-70348-9 (ebook)
Subjects: CYAC: Graphic novels. | Humorous stories. | Best friends—Fiction. | Friendship—Fiction. | Wrestling—Fiction. | Pizza—Fiction. | Tacos—Fiction. | LCGFT: Humorous comics. | Graphic novels.
Classification: LCC PZ7.7.S4548 Pjd 2024 (print) | LCC PZ7.7.S4548 (ebook) | DDC 741.5/973—dc23/eng/20230517

MANUFACTURED IN CHINA
10 9 8 7 6 5 4 3 2 1
First Edition

Contents

Chapter 1
Sports

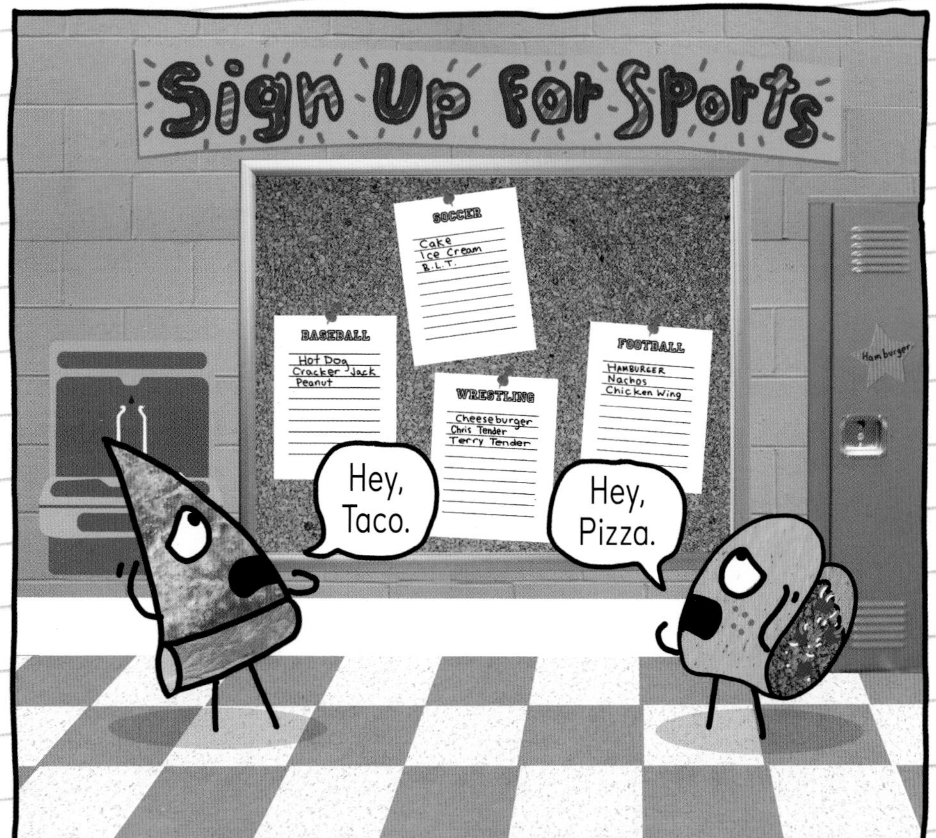
Sign Up for Sports
SOCCER
Cake
Ice Cream
B.L.T.
BASEBALL
Hot Dog
Cracker Jack
Peanut
WRESTLING
Cheeseburger
Chris Tender
Terry Tender
FOOTBALL
HAMBURGER
Nachos
Chicken Wing
Hamburger
Hey, Taco.
Hey, Pizza.

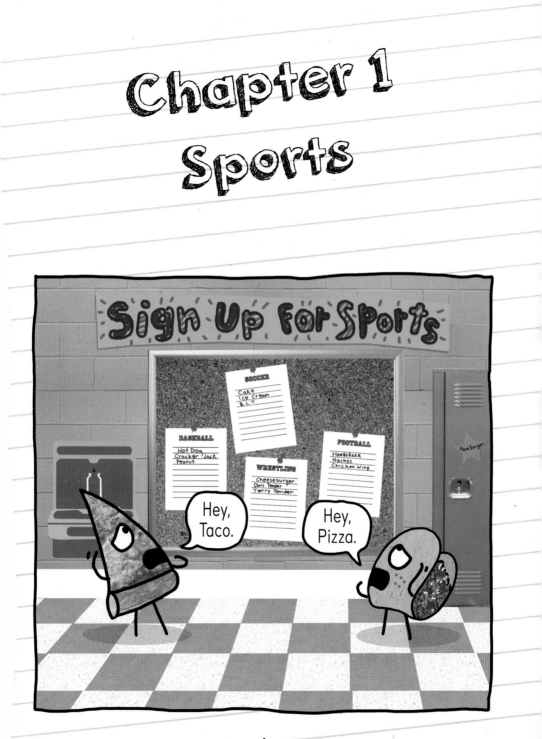

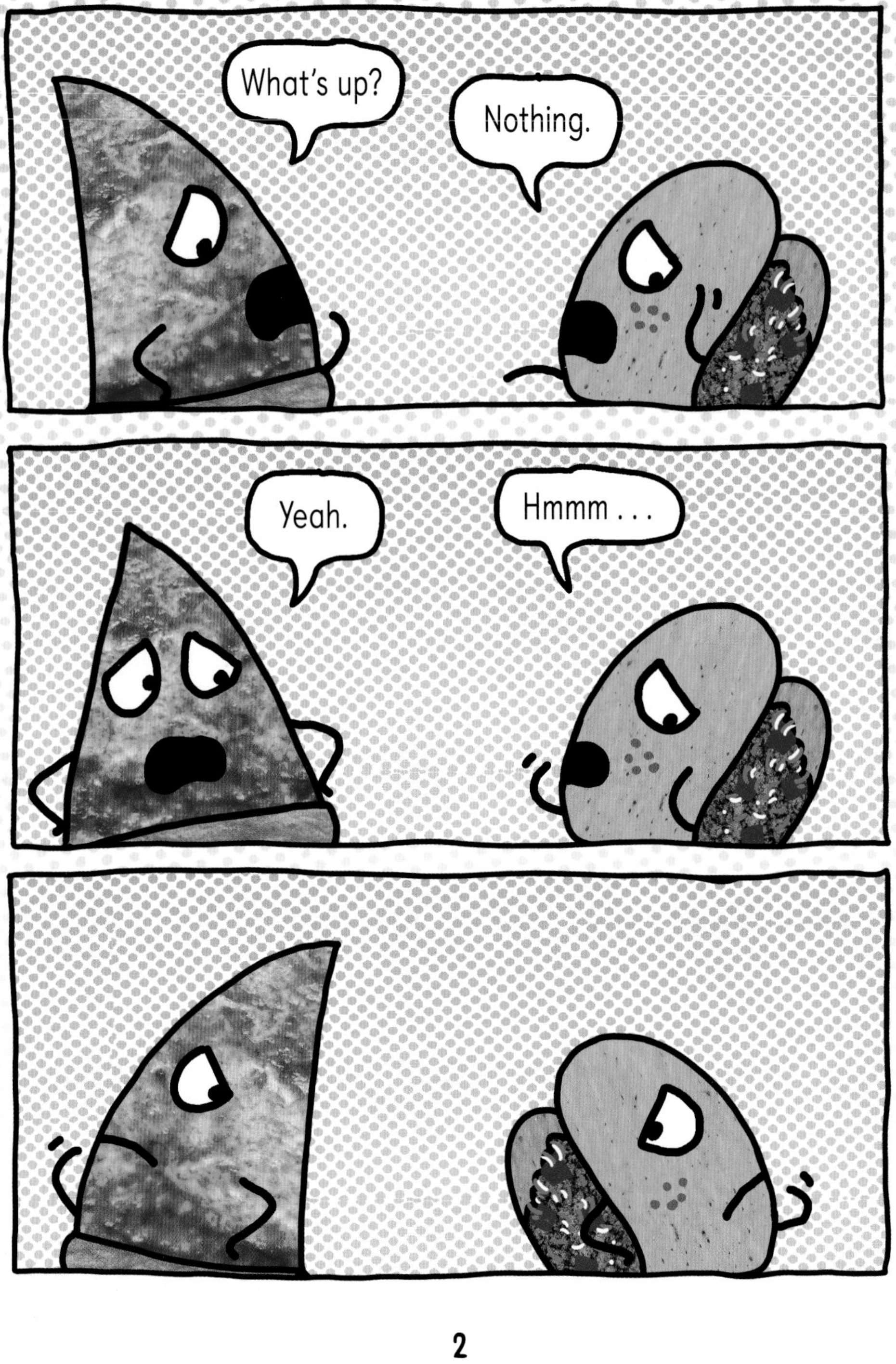
What's up?
Nothing.
Yeah.
Hmmm . . .

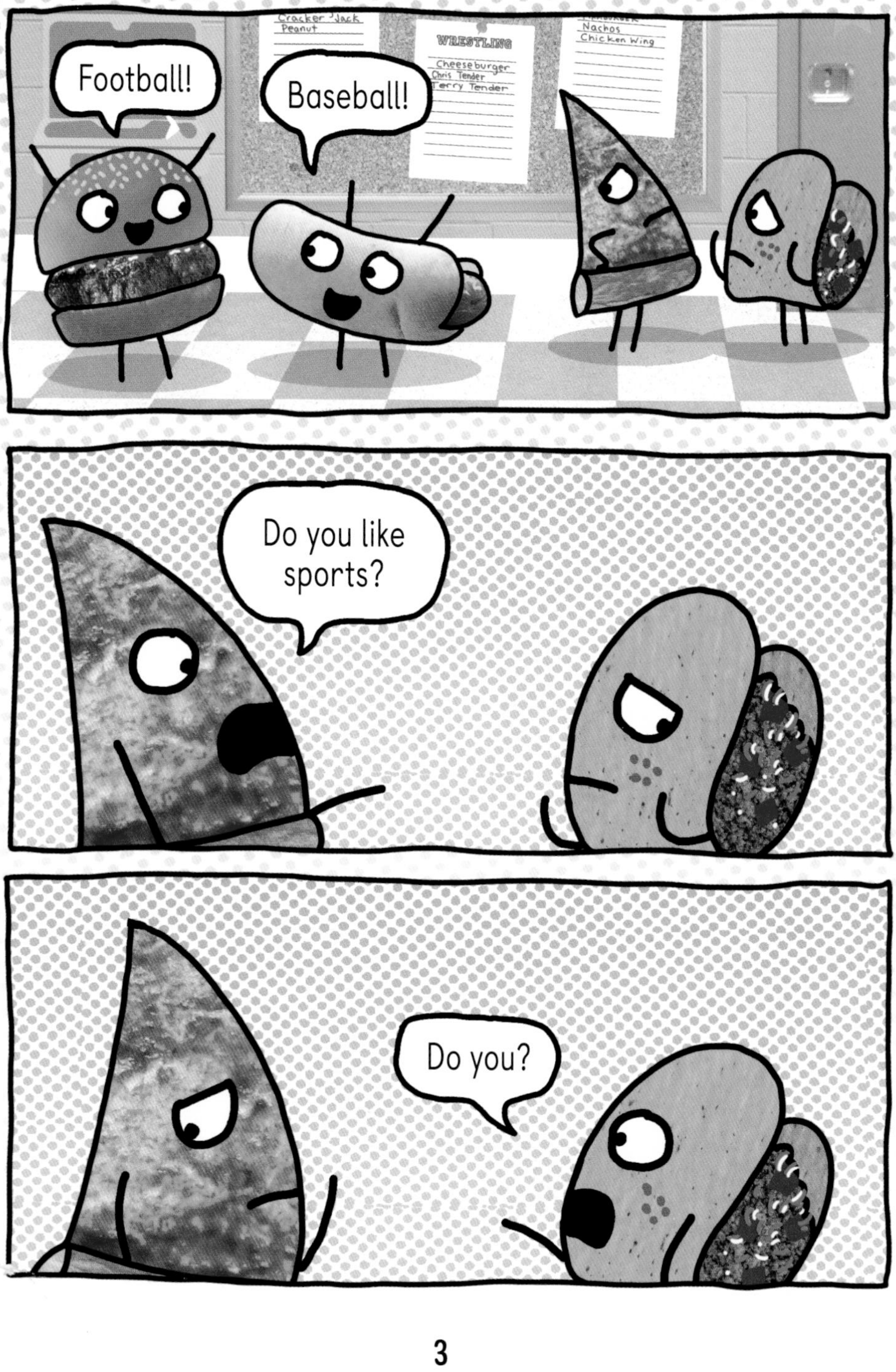
Cracker Jack
Peanut
WRESTLING
Cheeseburger
Chris Tender
Terry Tender
Nachos
Chicken Wing
Football!
Baseball!
Do you like sports?
Do you?

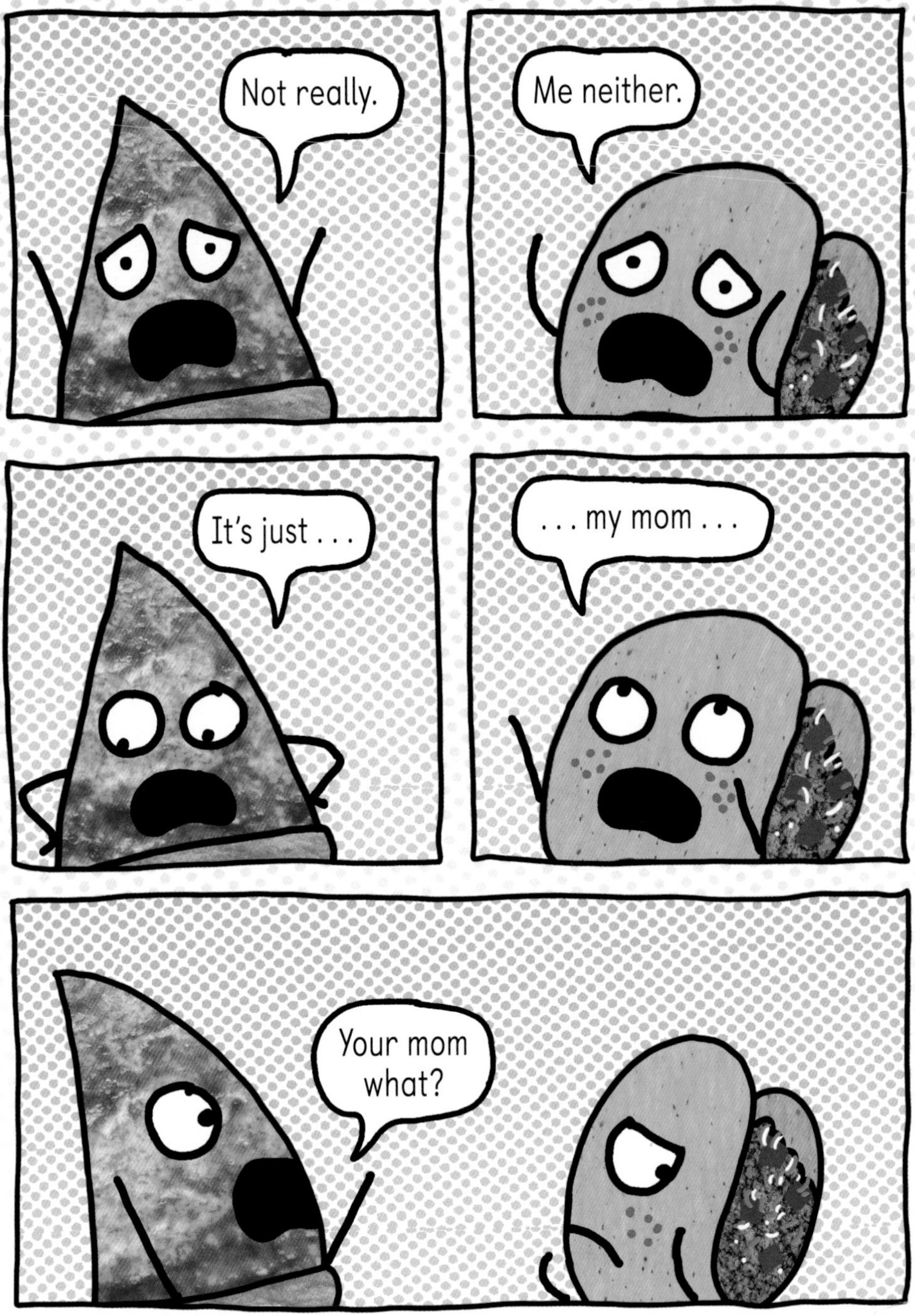
Not really.
Me neither.
It's just . . .
. . . my mom . . .
Your mom what?

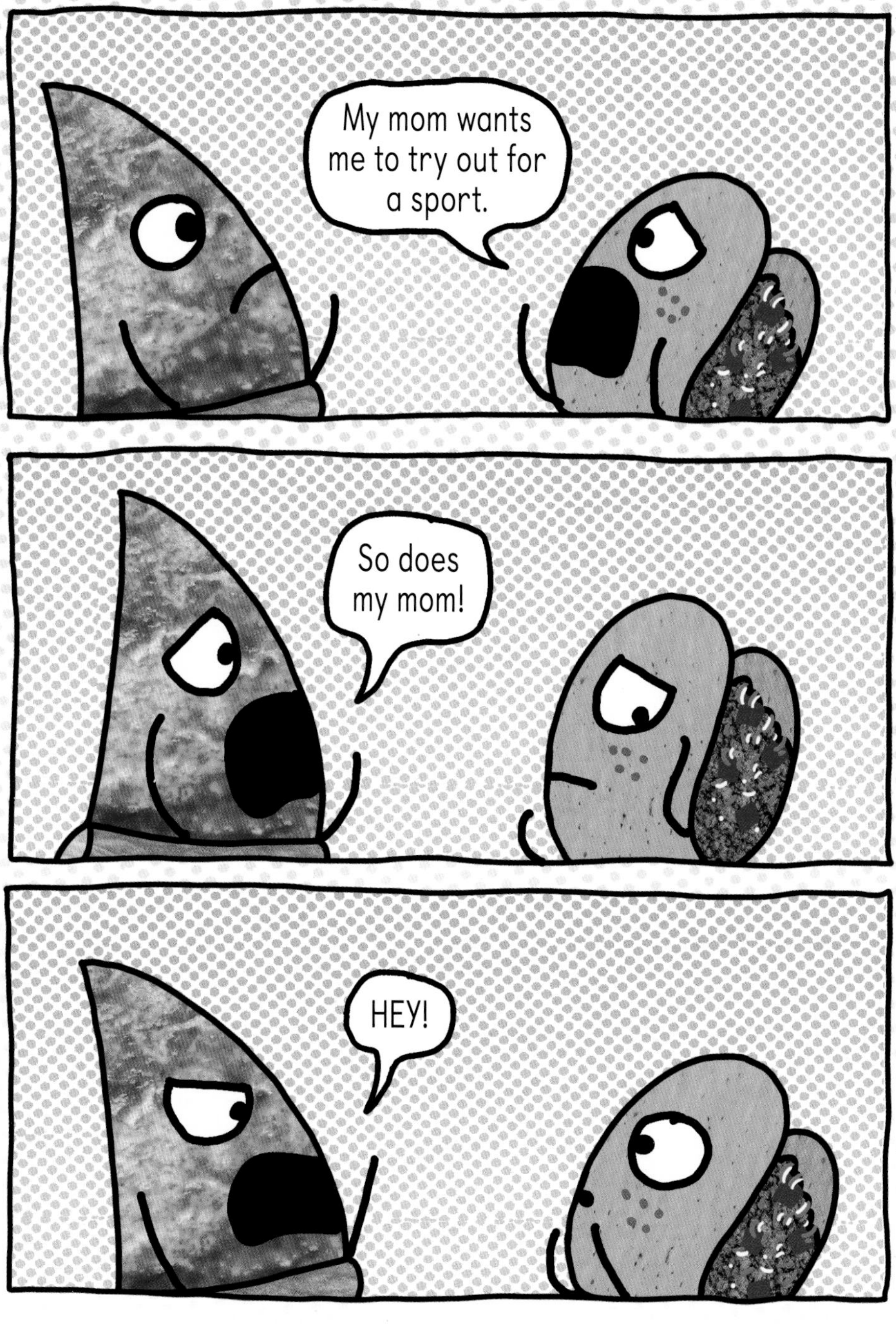
My mom wants me to try out for a sport.
So does my mom!
HEY!

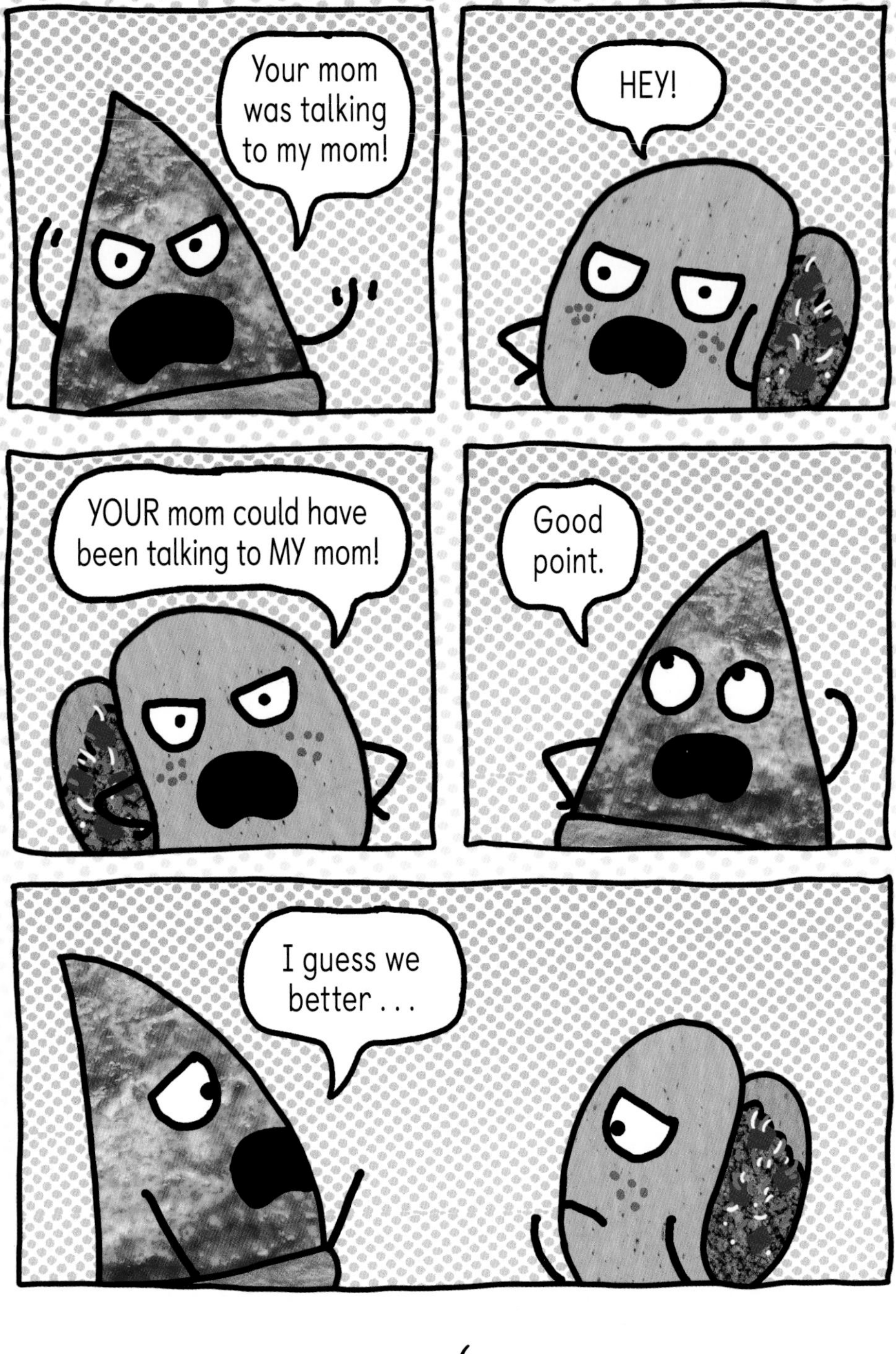
Your mom was talking to my mom!
HEY!
YOUR mom could have been talking to MY mom!
Good point.
I guess we better . . .

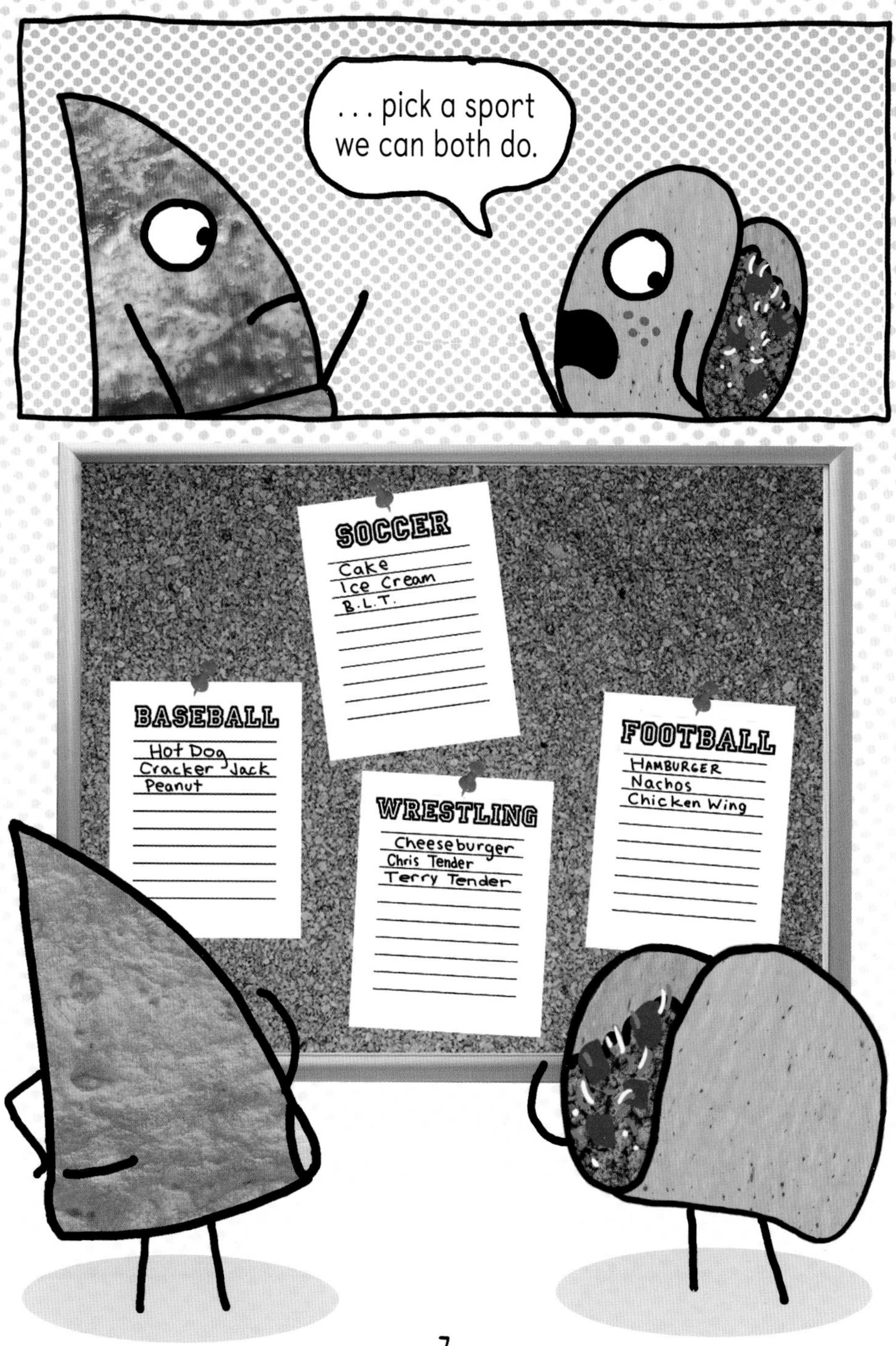
... pick a sport we can both do.
SOCCER
Cake
Ice Cream
B.L.T.
BASEBALL
Hot Dog
Cracker Jack
Peanut
WRESTLING
Cheeseburger
Chris Tender
Terry Tender
FOOTBALL
HAMBURGER
Nachos
Chicken Wing

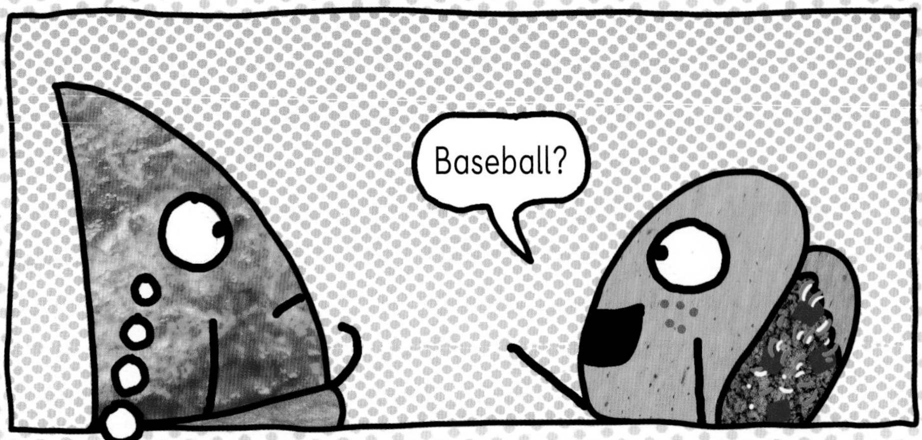
Baseball?

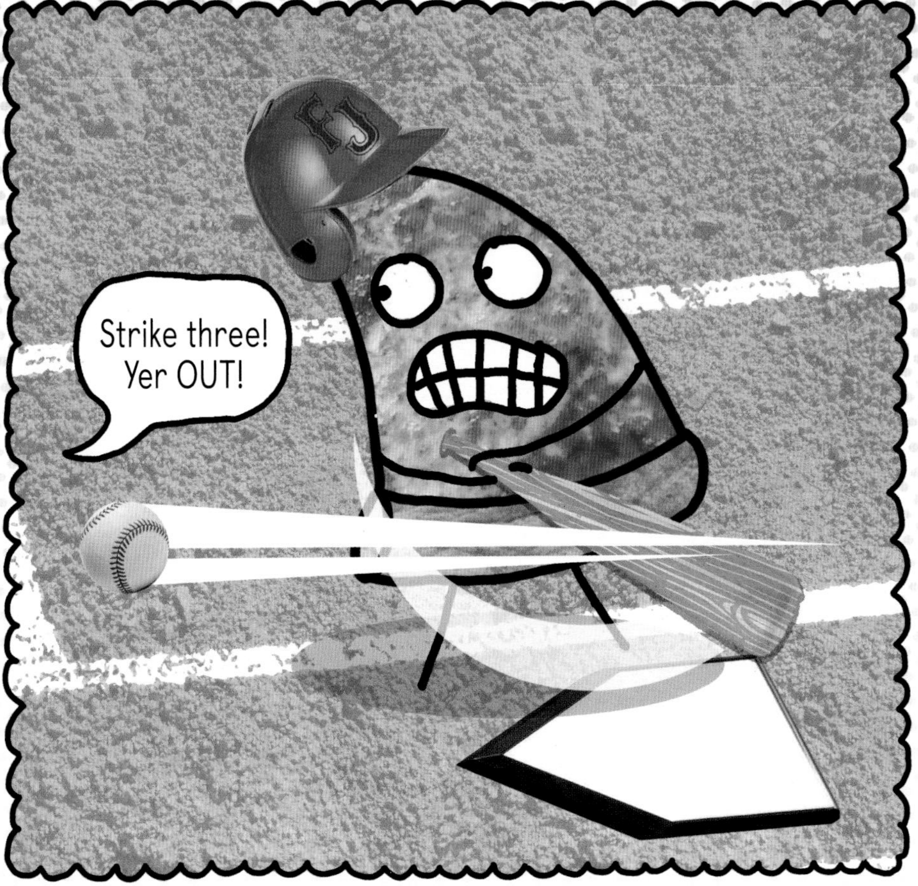
Strike three!
Yer OUT!

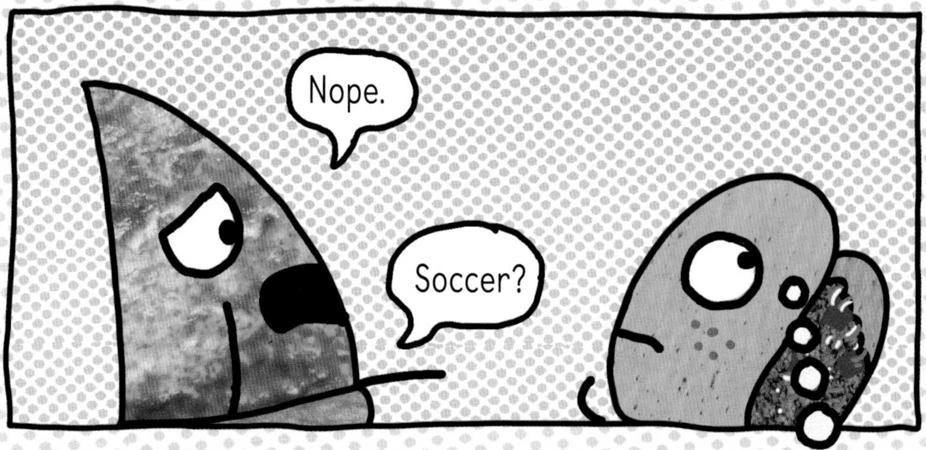
Nope.
Soccer?

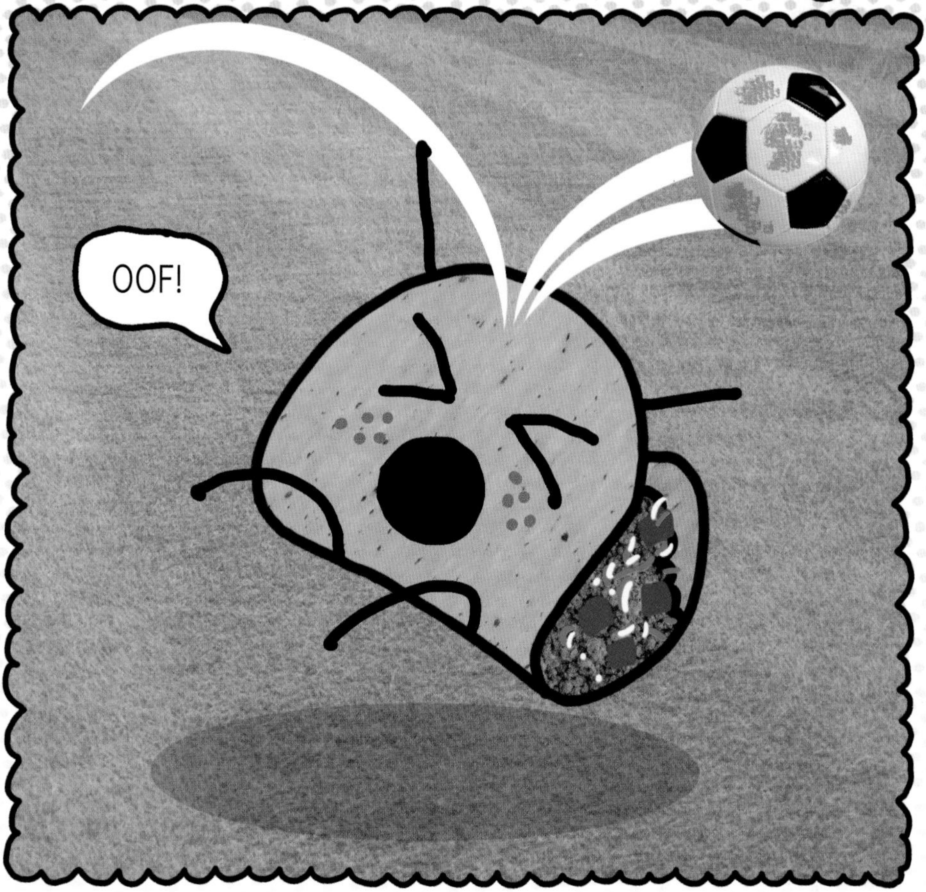
OOF!

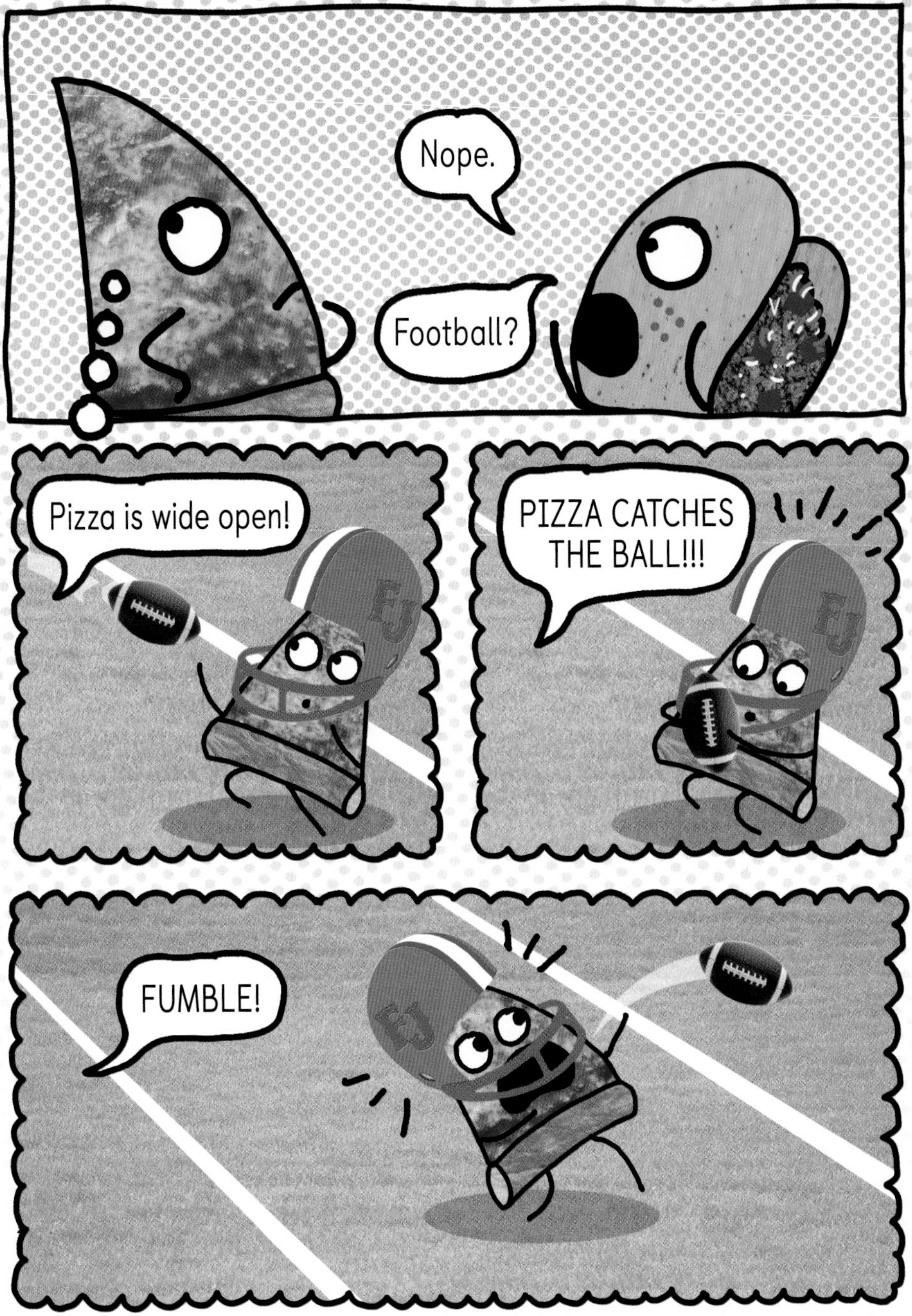
Nope.
Football?
Pizza is wide open!
PIZZA CATCHES THE BALL!!!
FUMBLE!

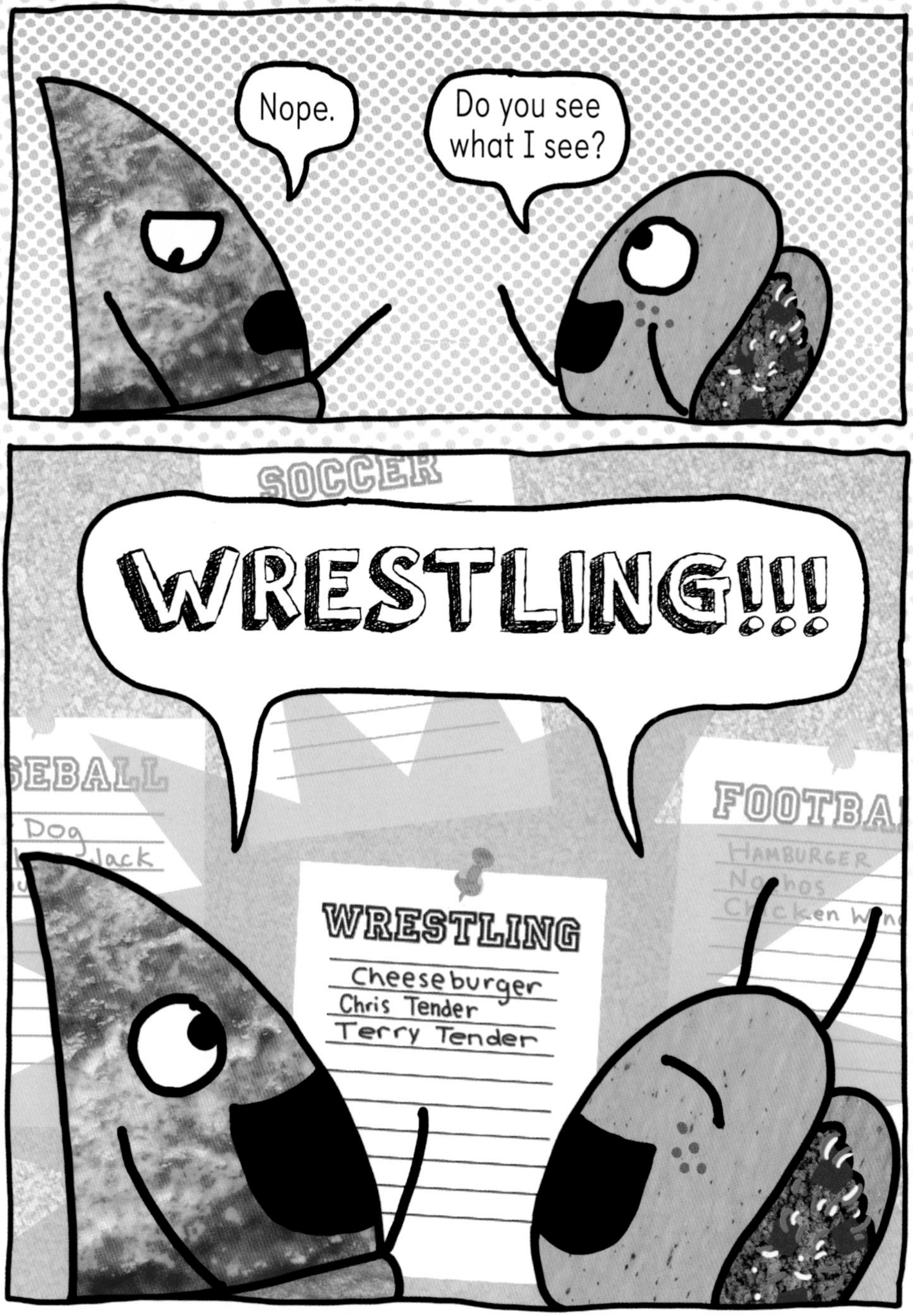
Nope.
Do you see what I see?
SOCCER
WRESTLING!!!
WRESTLING
Cheeseburger
Chris Tender
Terry Tender
HAMBURGER

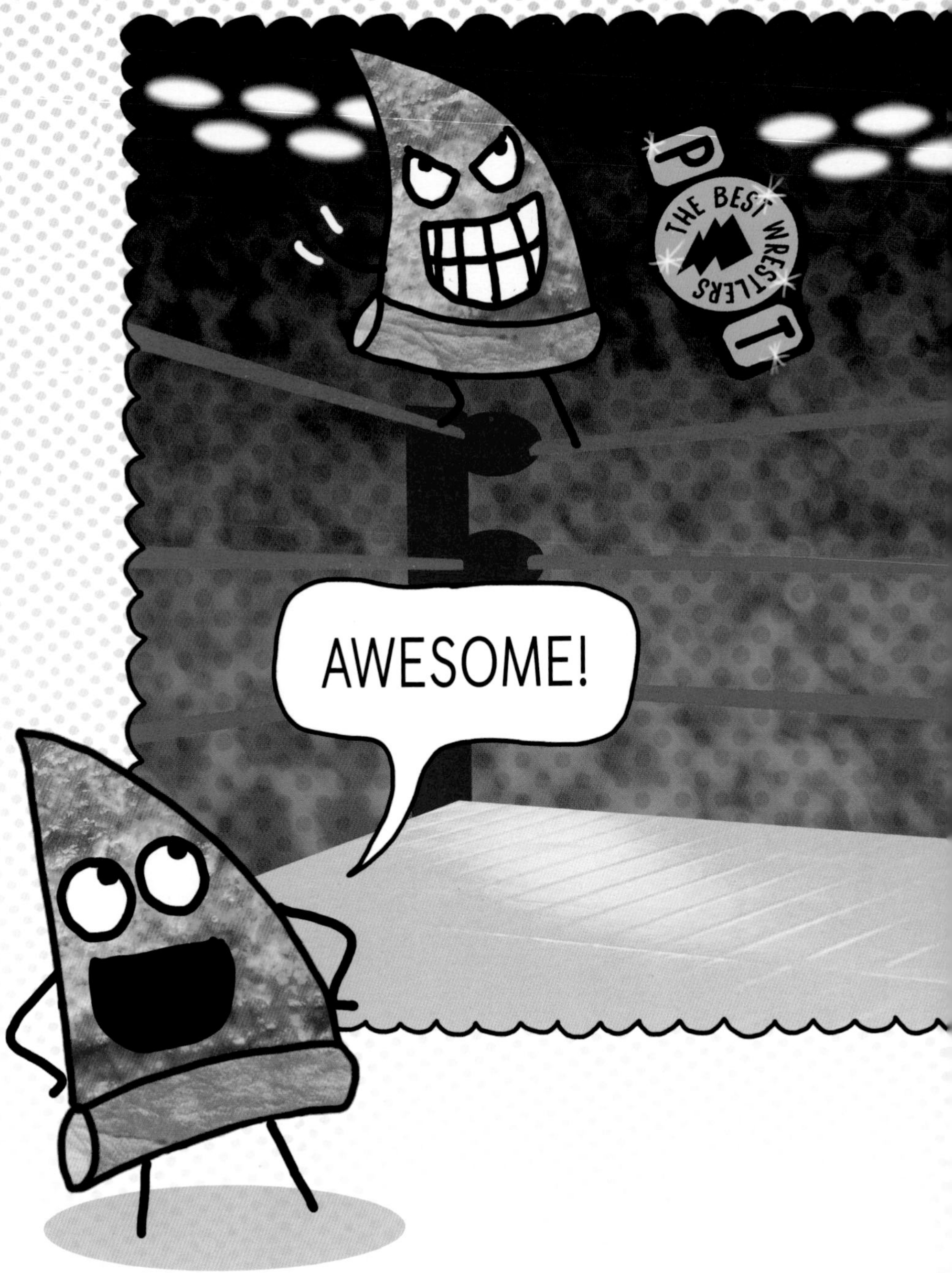
P
THE BEST WRESTLERS
T
AWESOME!

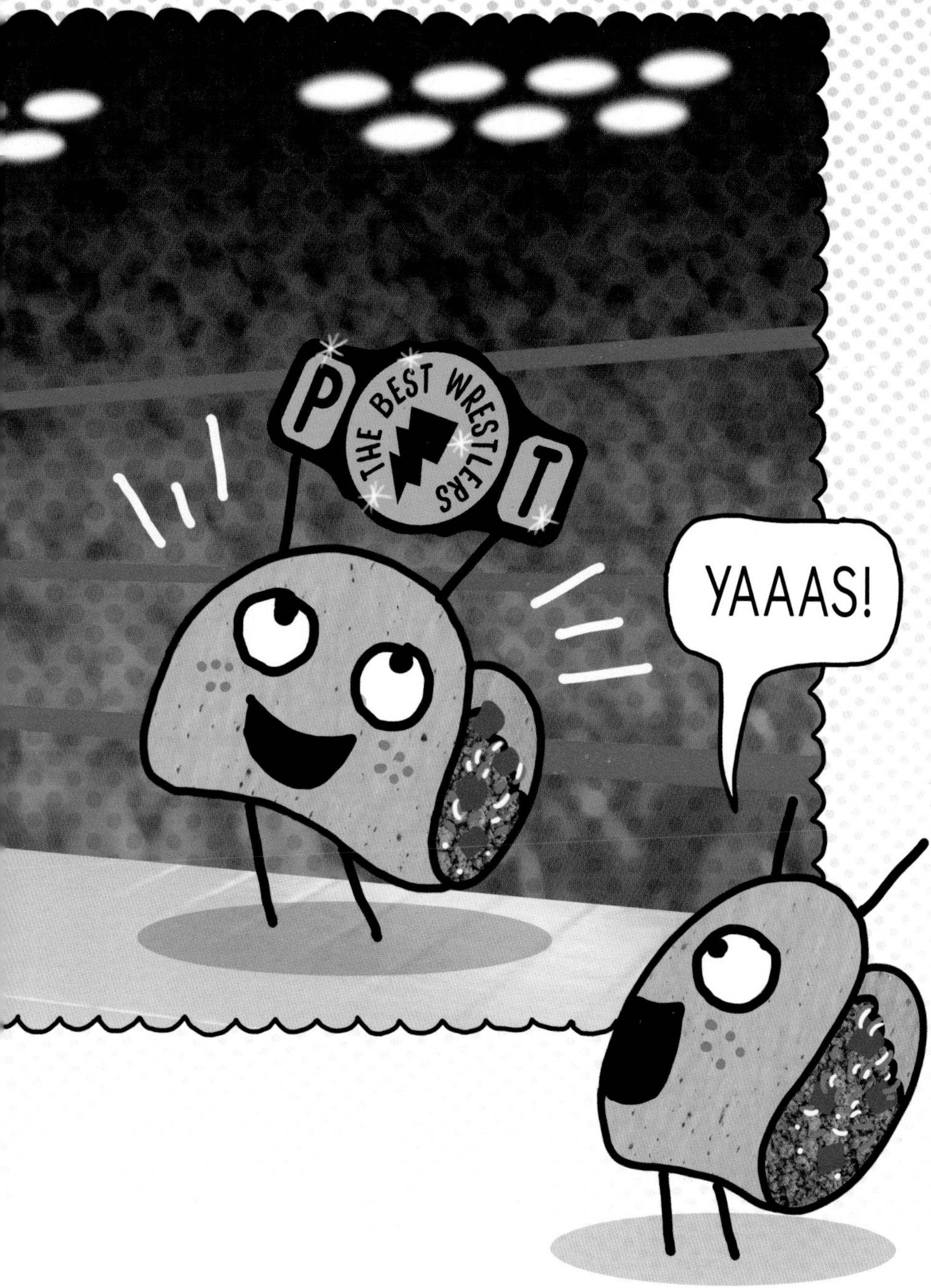
P
THE BEST WRESTLERS
T
YAAAS!

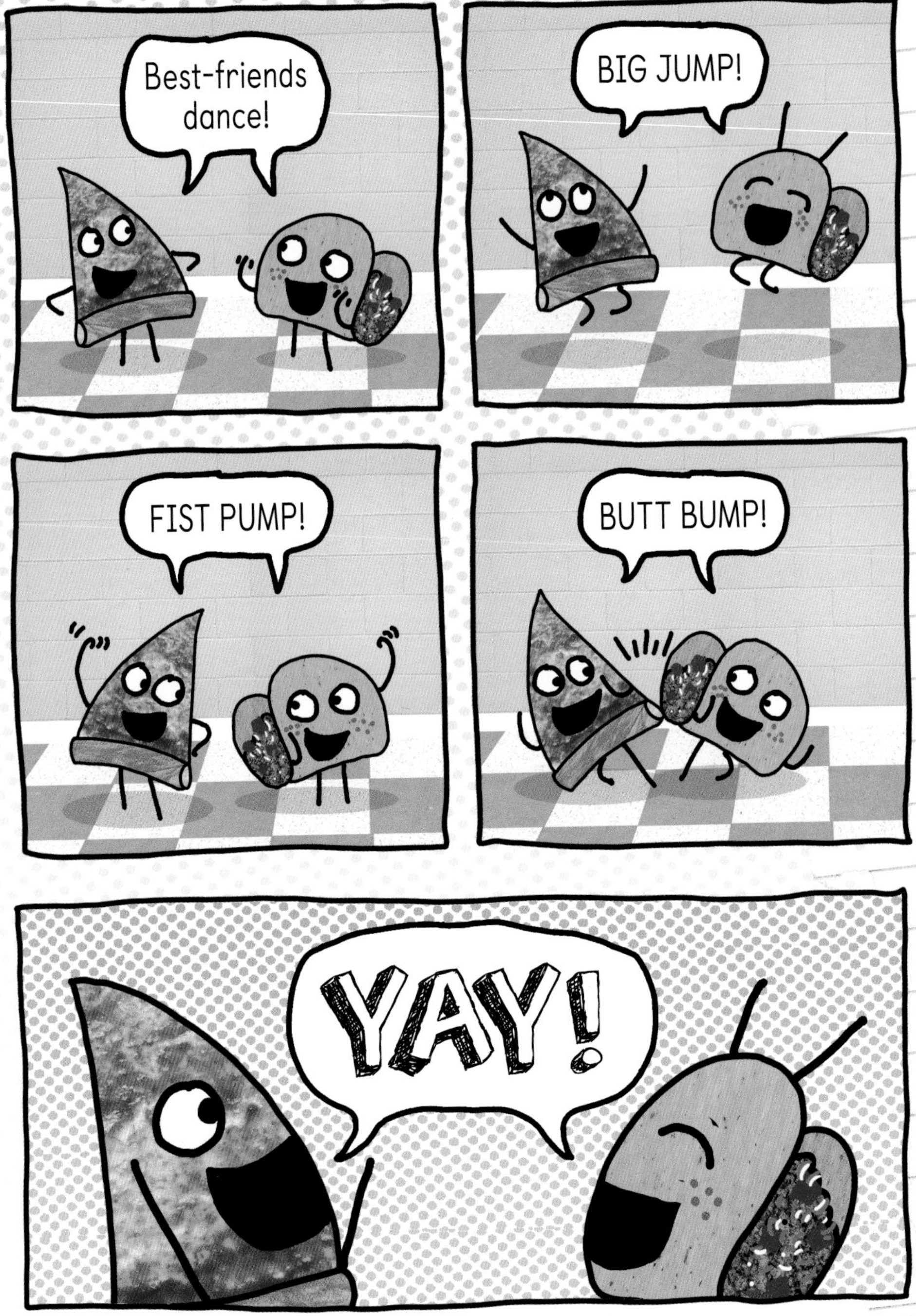
Best-friends dance!
BIG JUMP!
FIST PUMP!
BUTT BUMP!
YAY!

Chapter 2
Favorite Wrestlers

Media Center
BASEBALL
Hot Dog
Cracker Jack
Peanut
Who's your favorite wrestler?

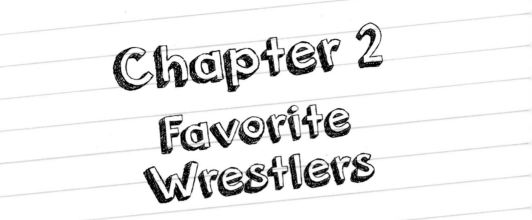

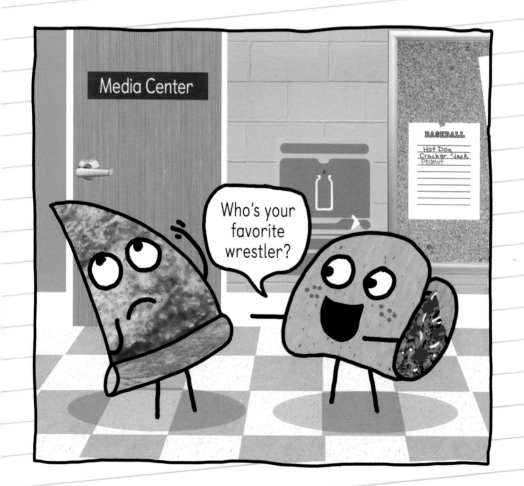

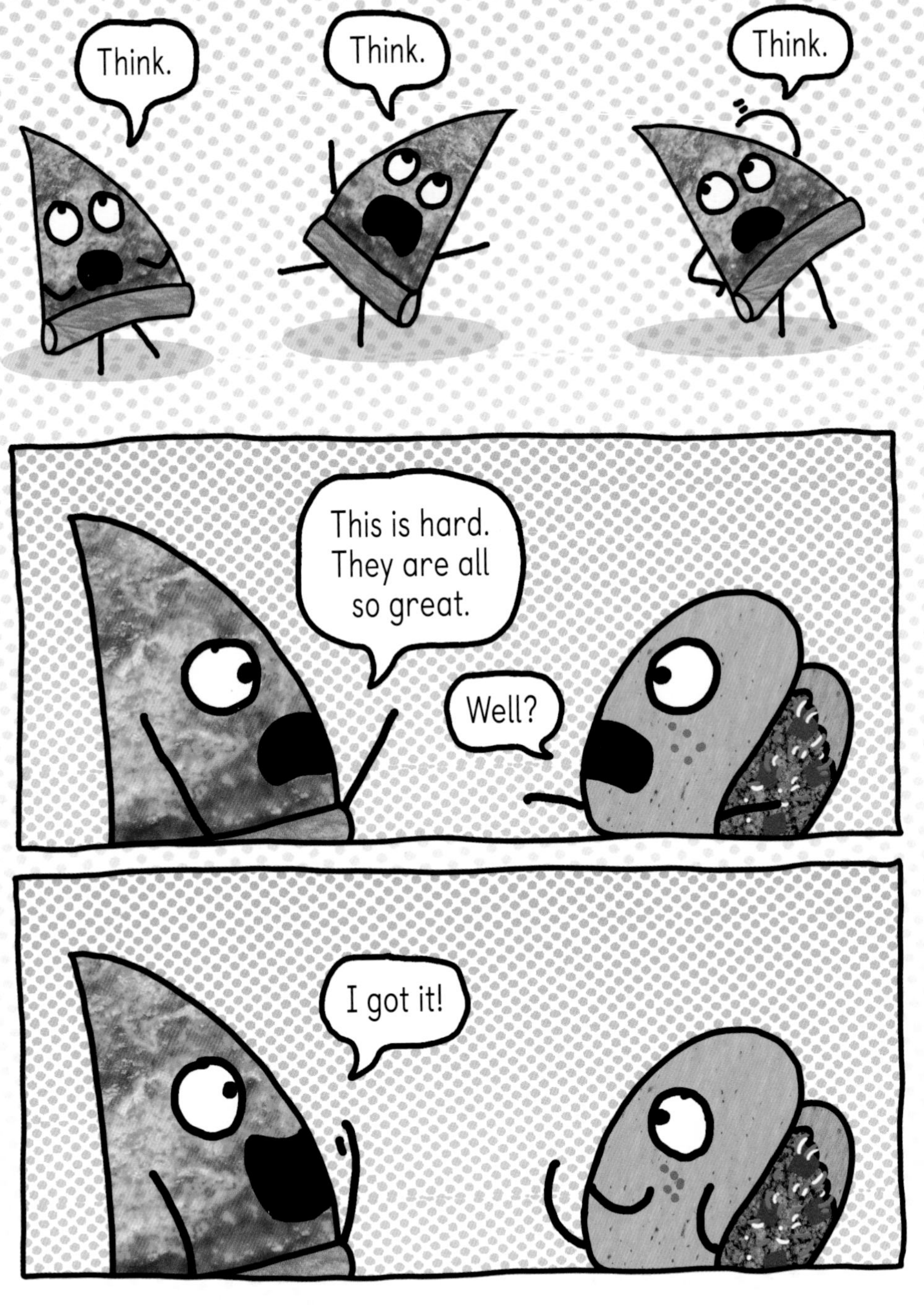
Think.
Think.
Think.
This is hard. They are all so great.
Well?
I got it!

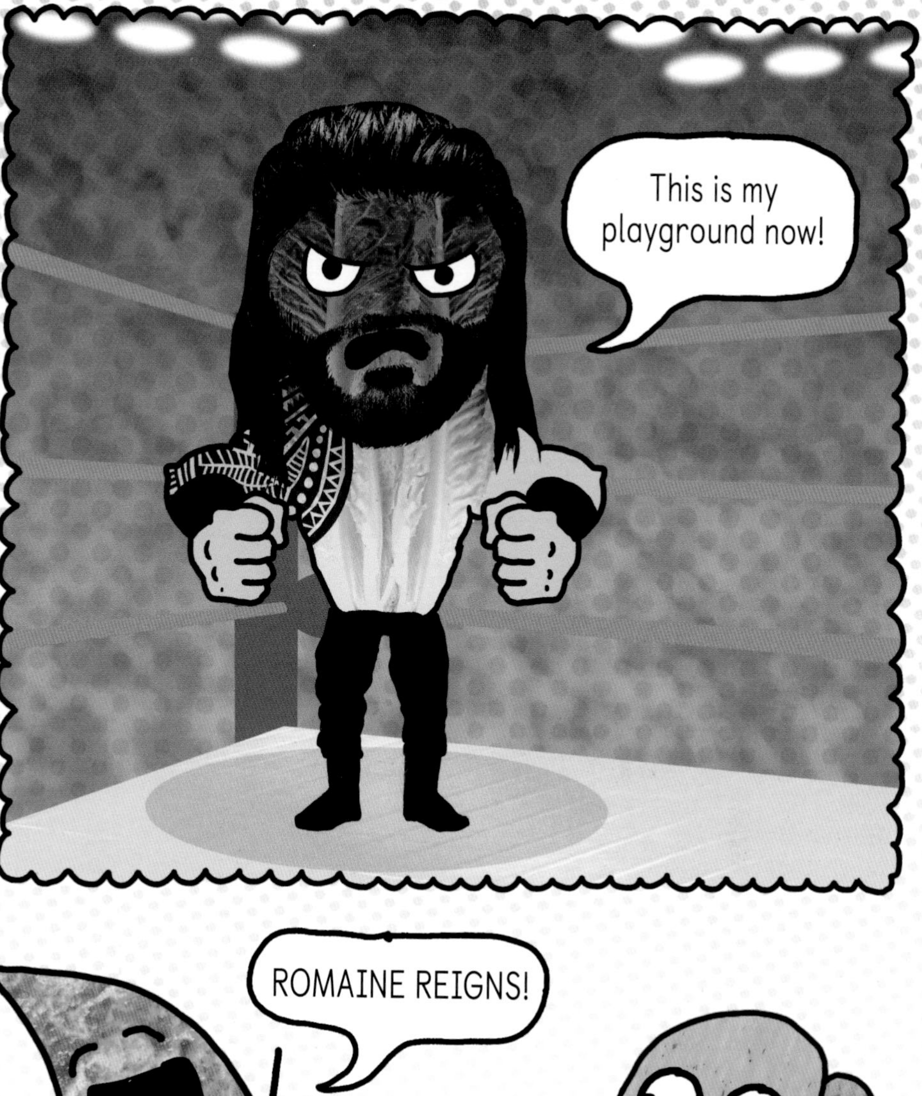
This is my playground now!

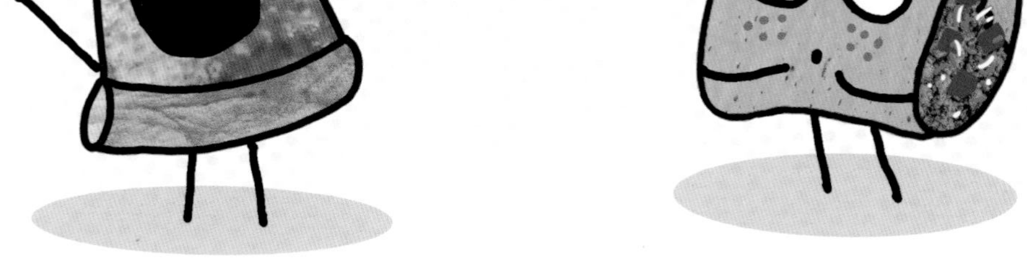
ROMAINE REIGNS!

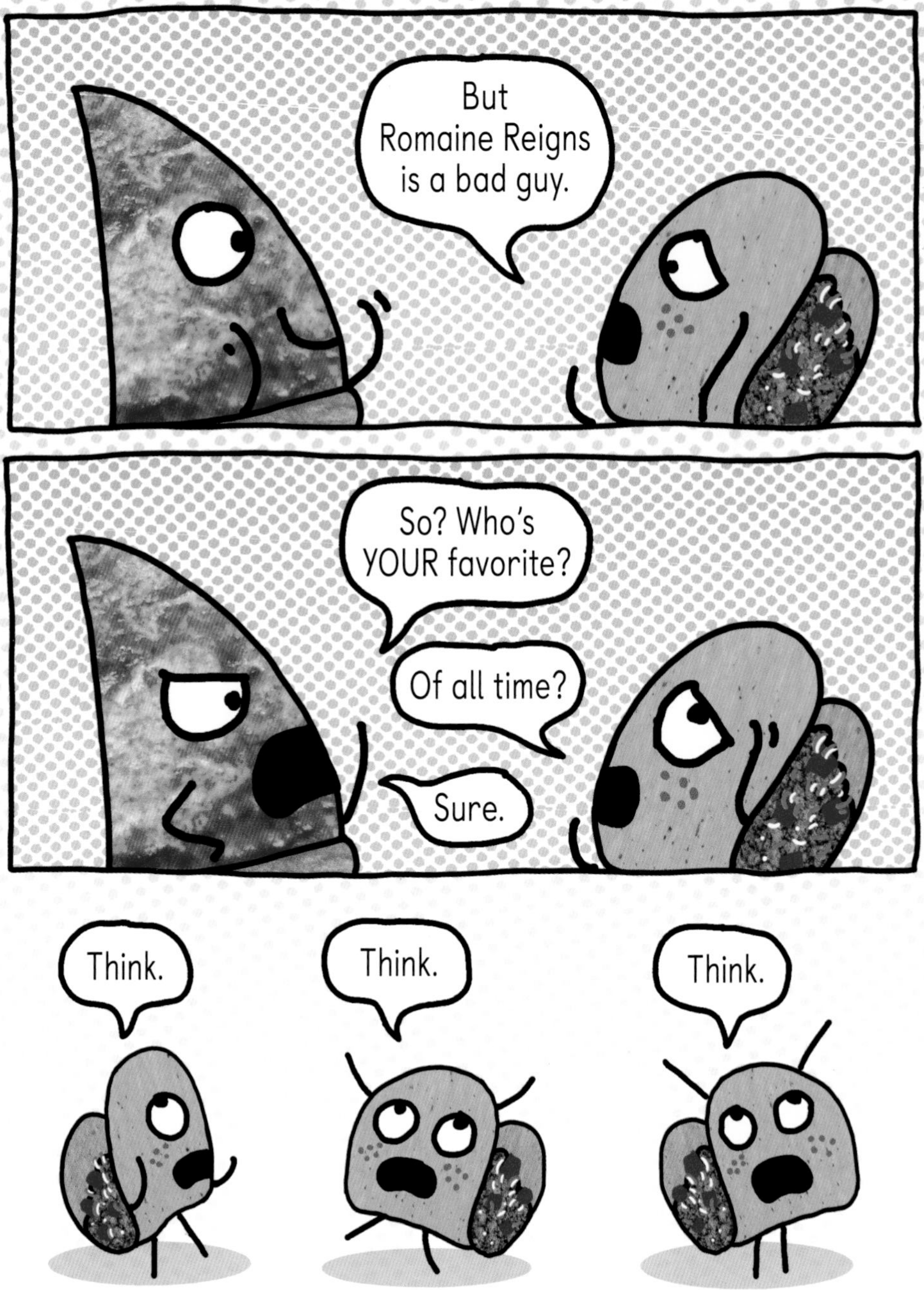
But Romaine Reigns is a bad guy.
So? Who's YOUR favorite?
Of all time?
Sure.
Think.
Think.
Think.

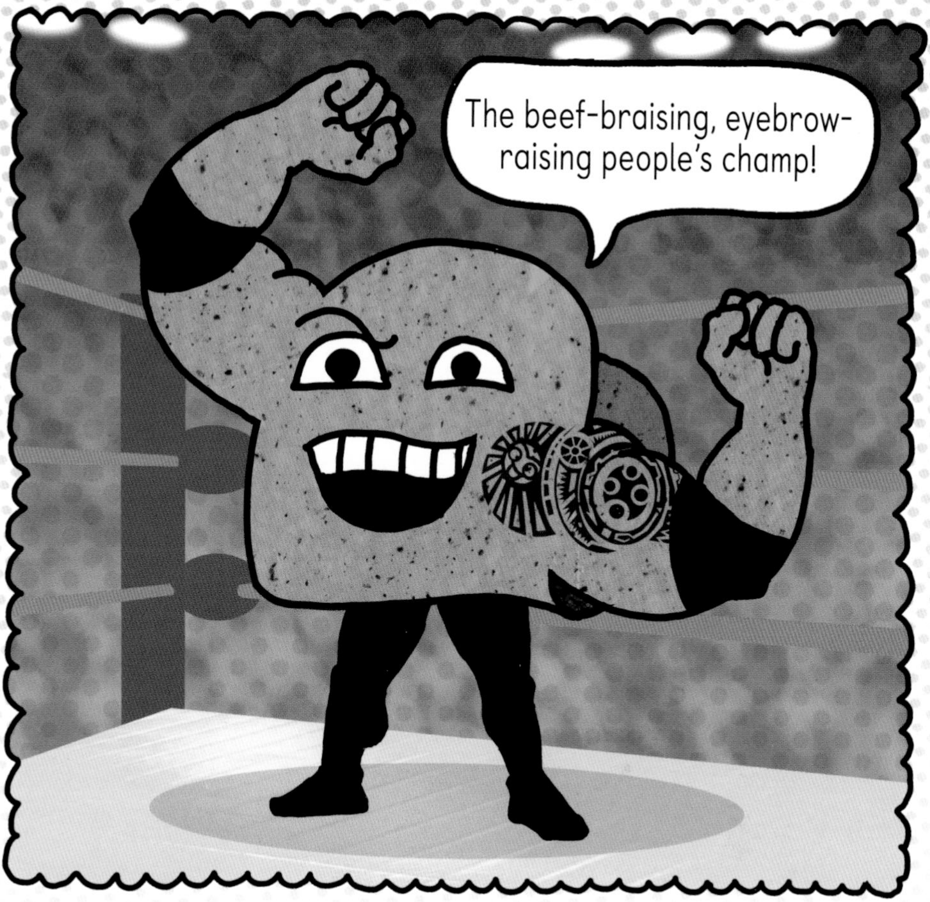
The beef-braising, eyebrow-raising people's champ!

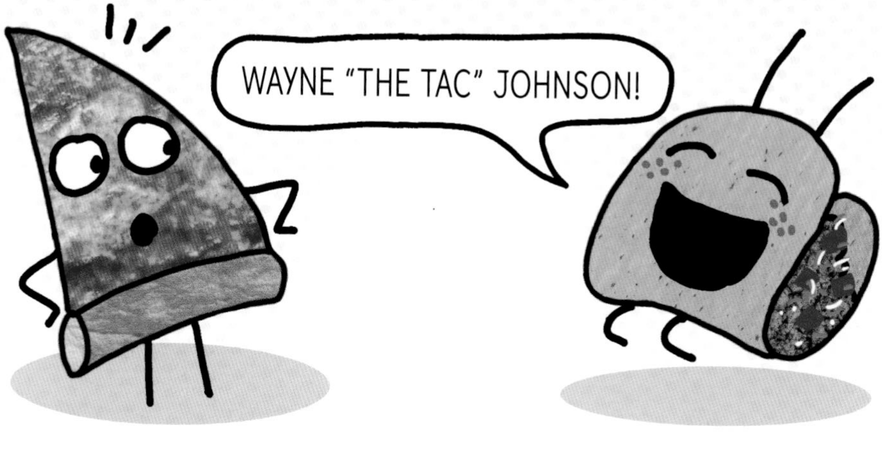
WAYNE "THE TAC" JOHNSON!

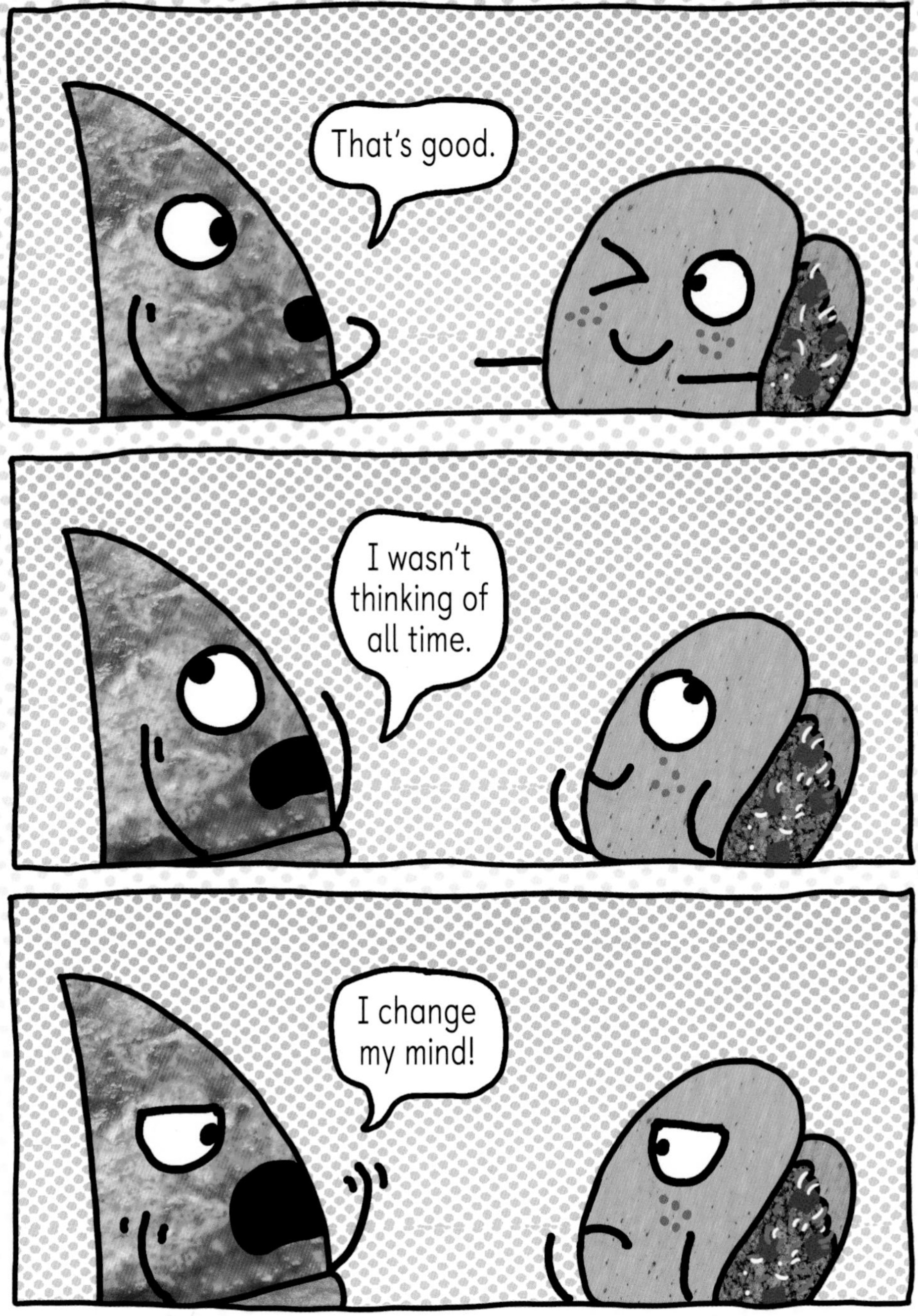
That's good.
I wasn't thinking of all time.
I change my mind!

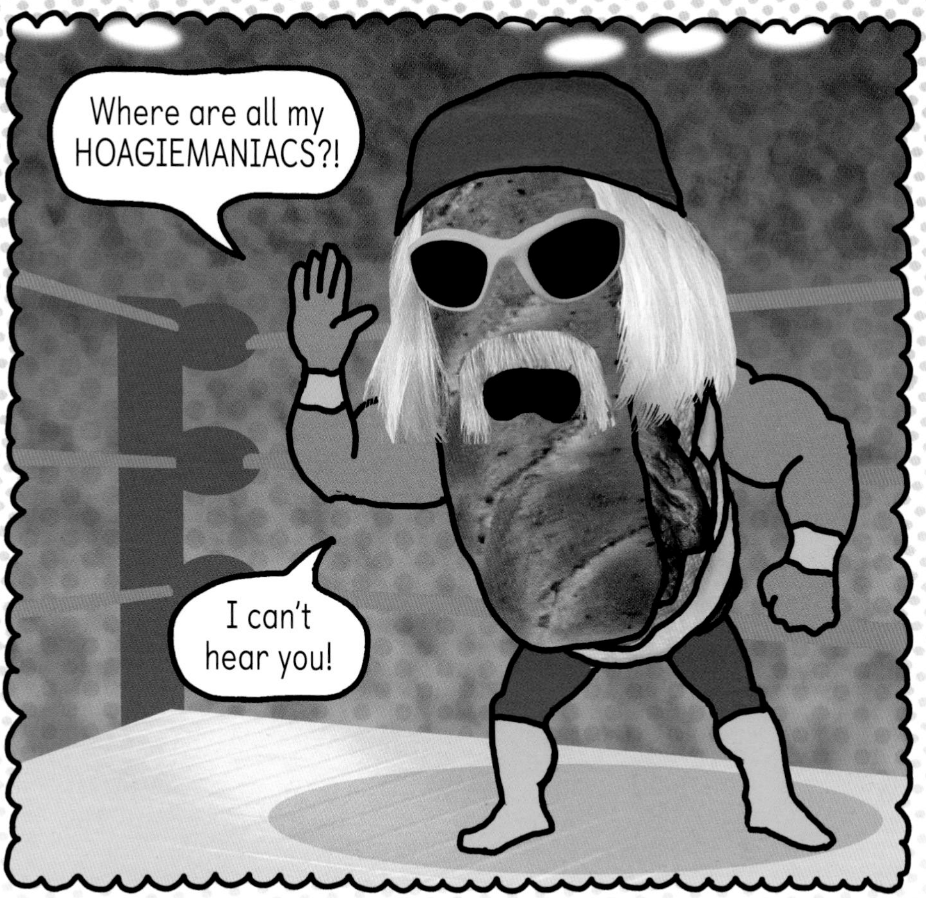
Where are all my HOAGIEMANIACS?!
I can't hear you!

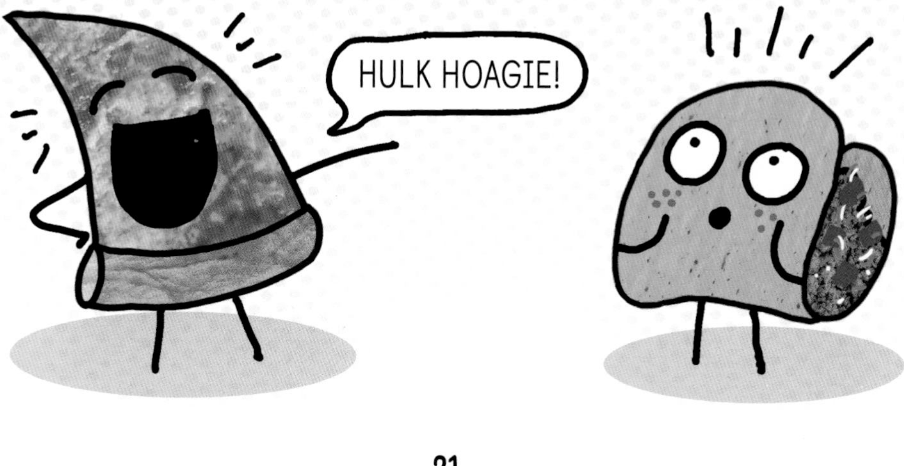
HULK HOAGIE!

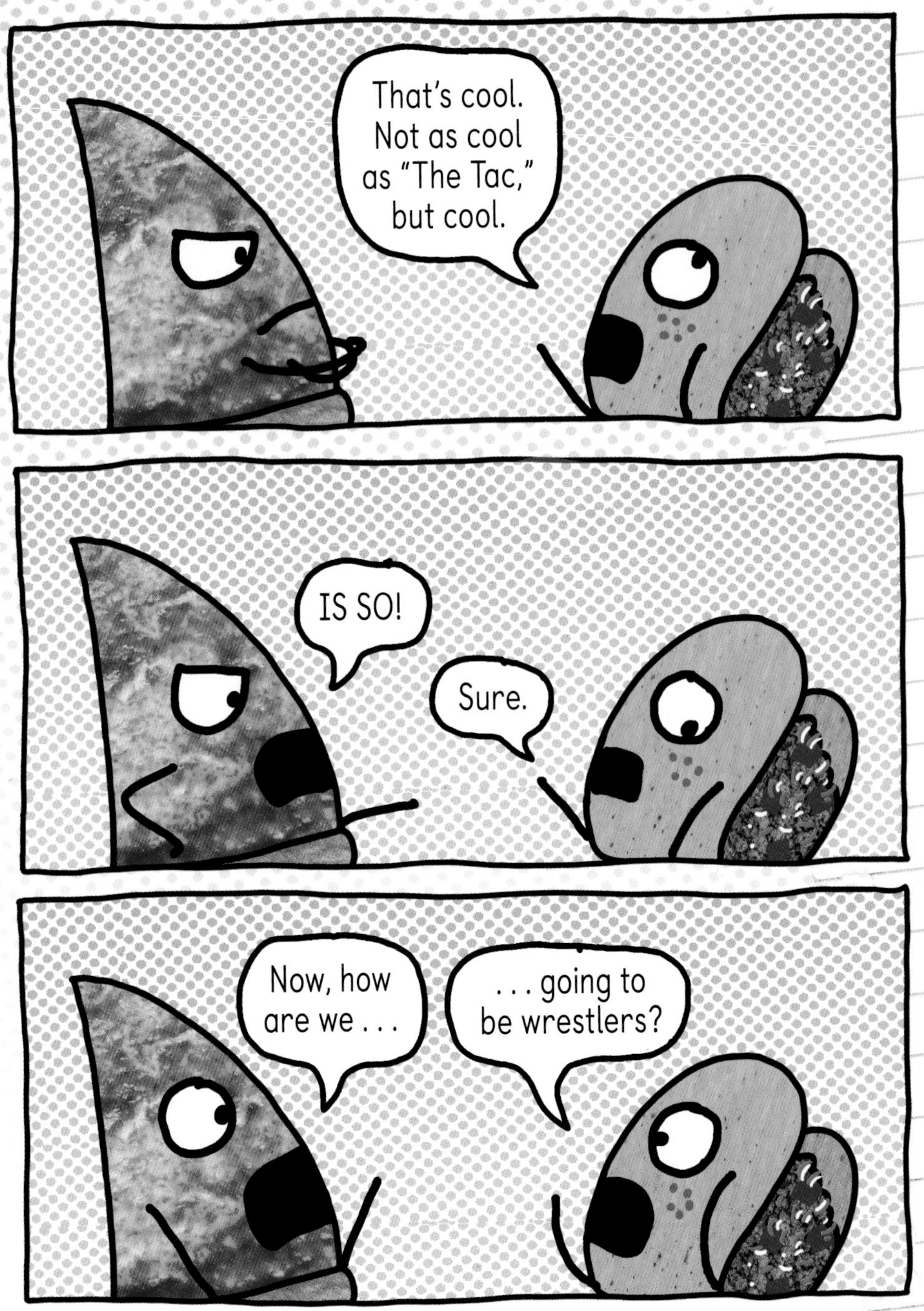
That's cool. Not as cool as "The Tac," but cool.
IS SO!
Sure.
Now, how are we . . .
. . . going to be wrestlers?

Chapter 3
How to Be a Wrestler

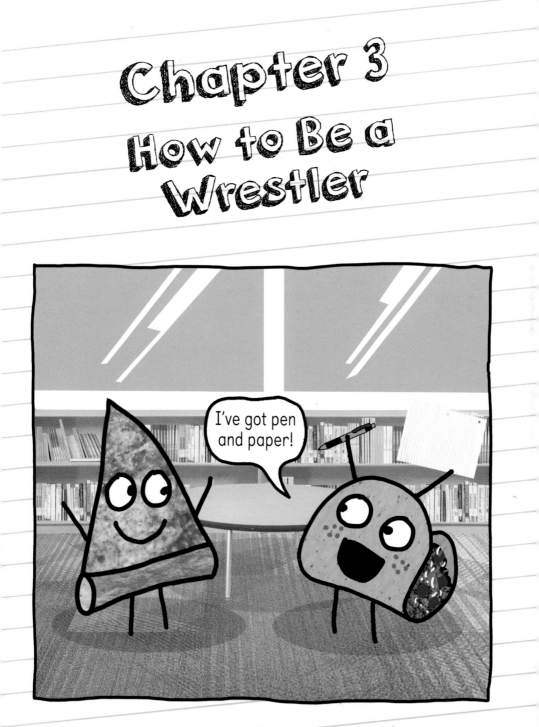

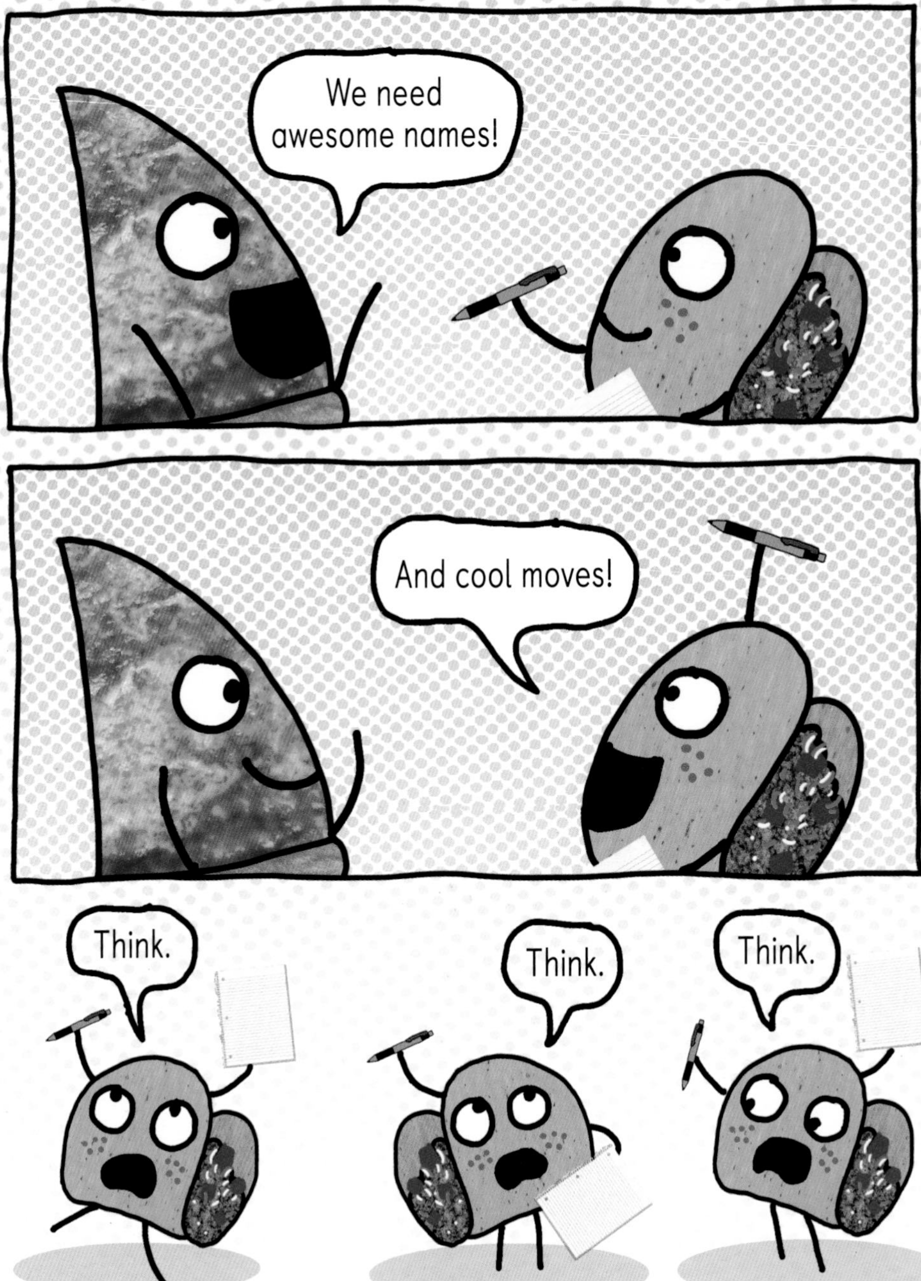
We need awesome names!
And cool moves!
Think.
Think.
Think.

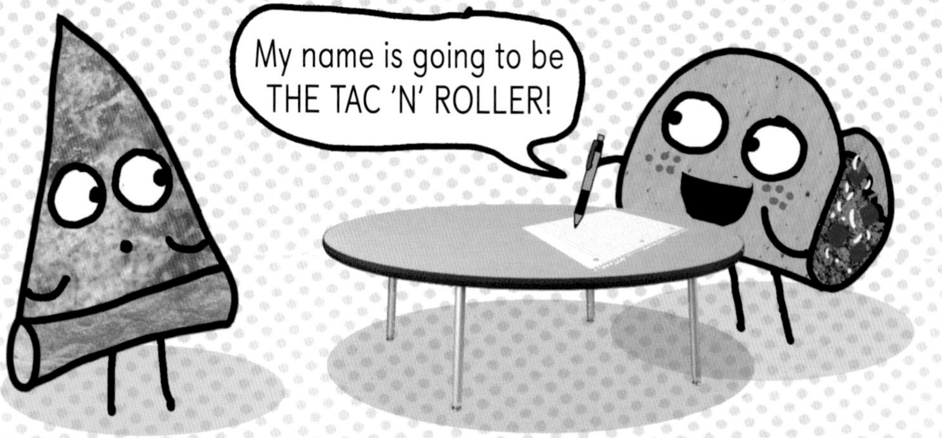
My name is going to be THE TAC 'N' ROLLER!

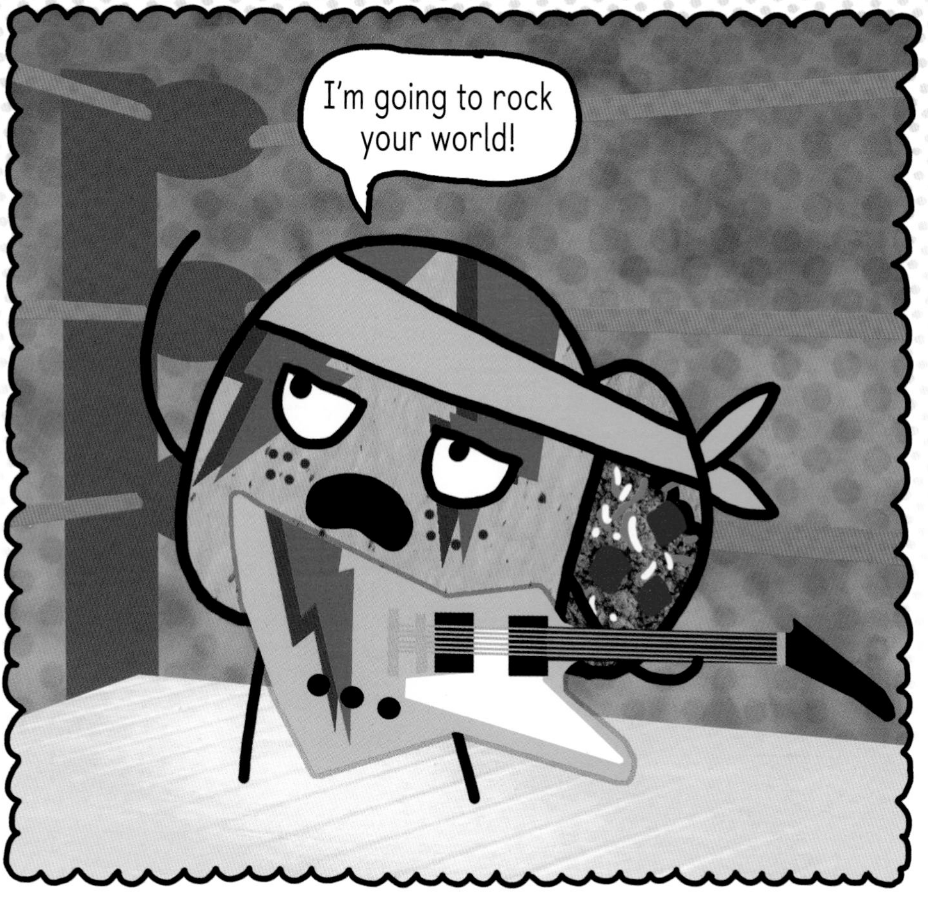
I'm going to rock your world!

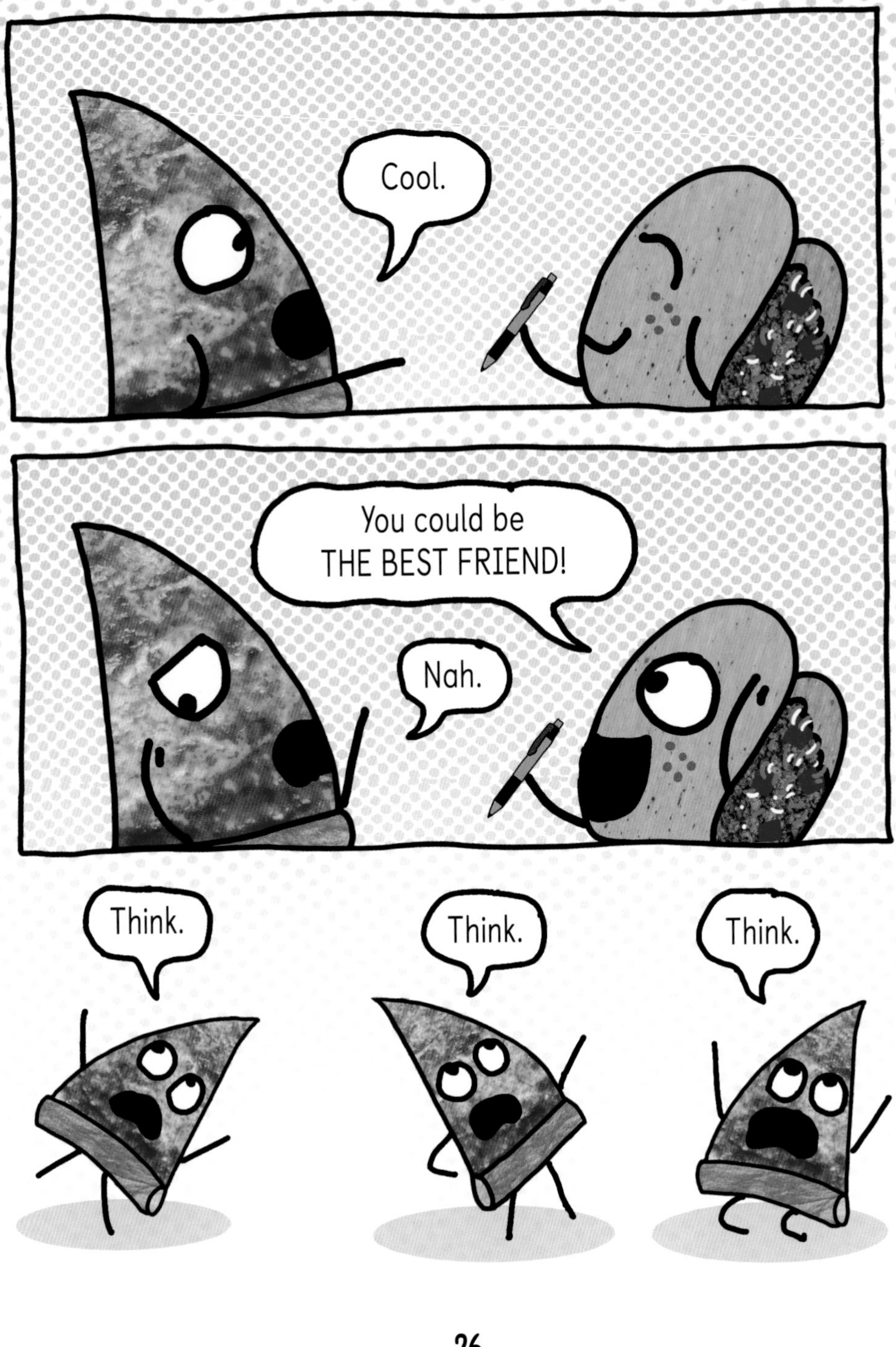
Cool.
You could be THE BEST FRIEND!
Nah.
Think.
Think.
Think.

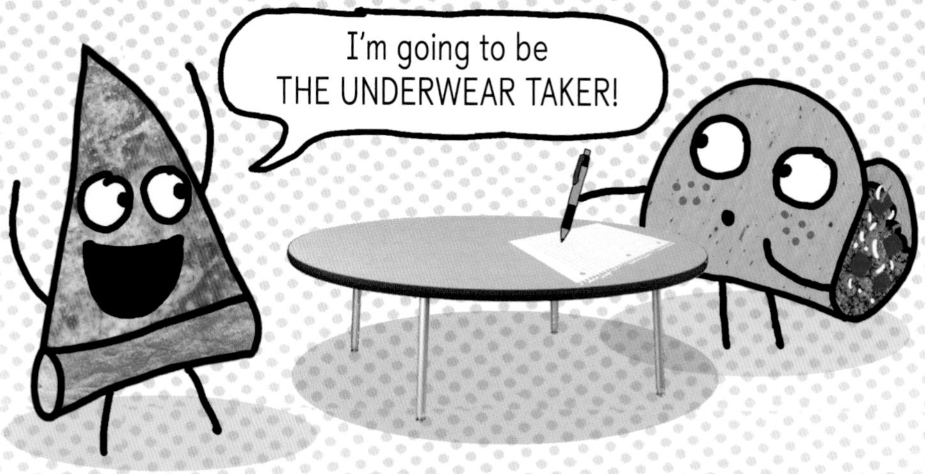
I'm going to be THE UNDERWEAR TAKER!

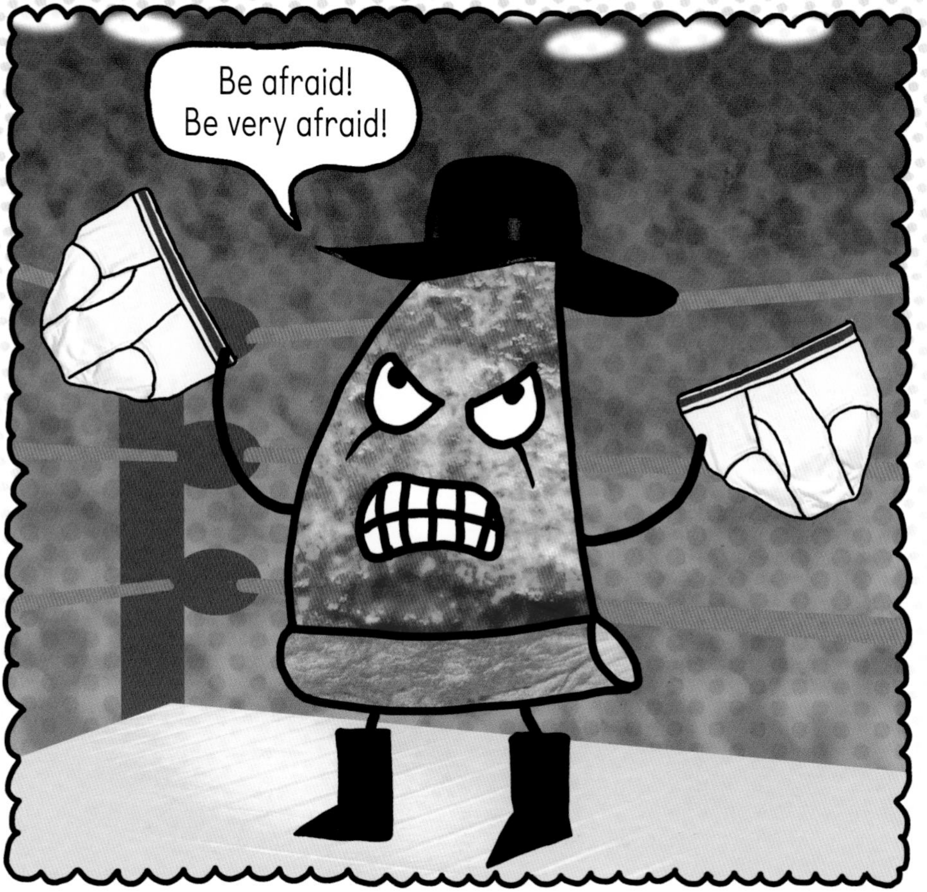
Be afraid! Be very afraid!

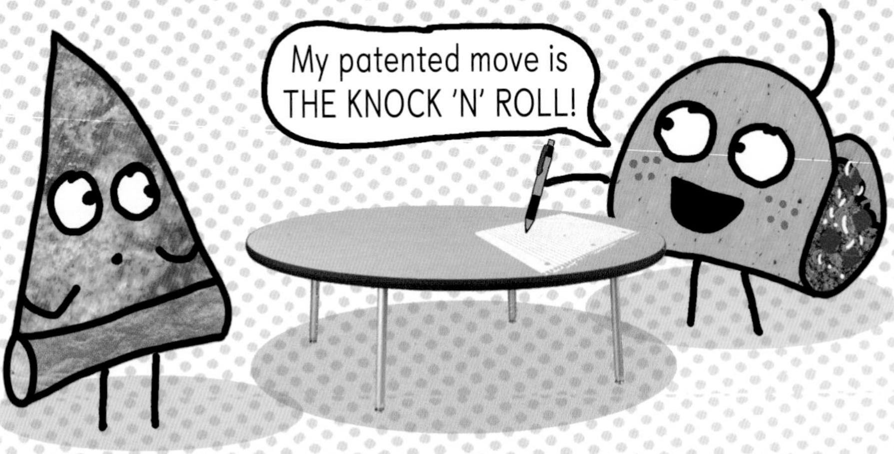
My patented move is THE KNOCK 'N' ROLL!

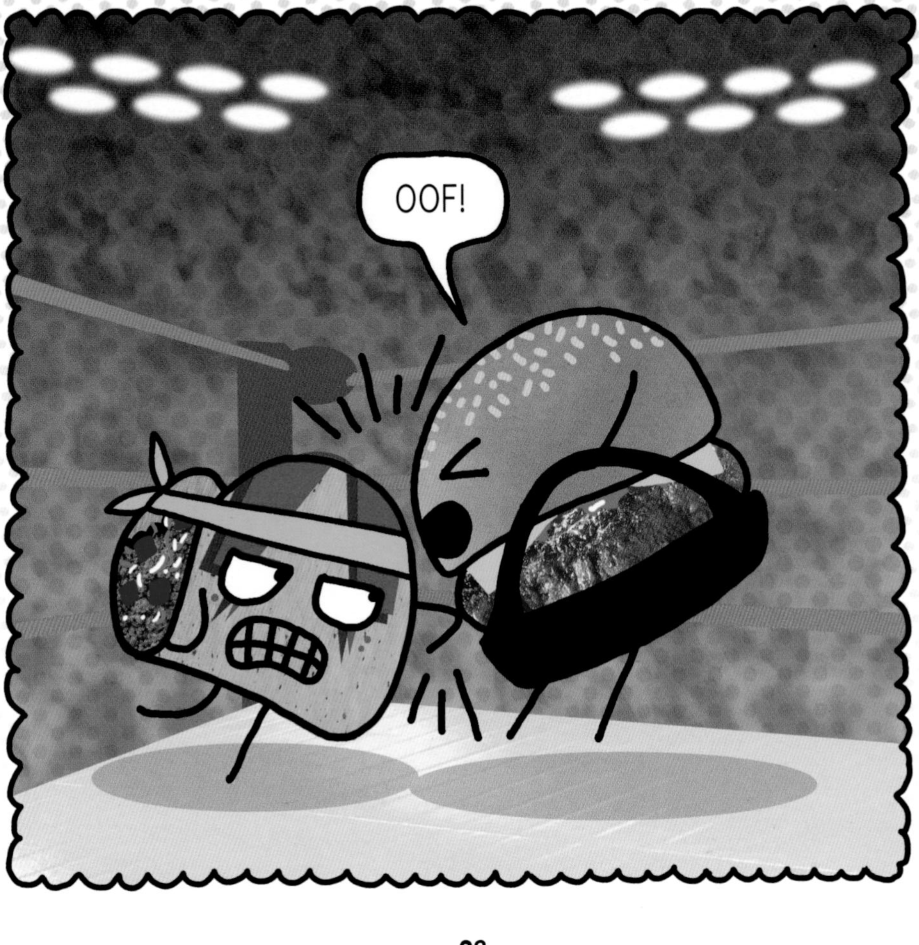
OOF!

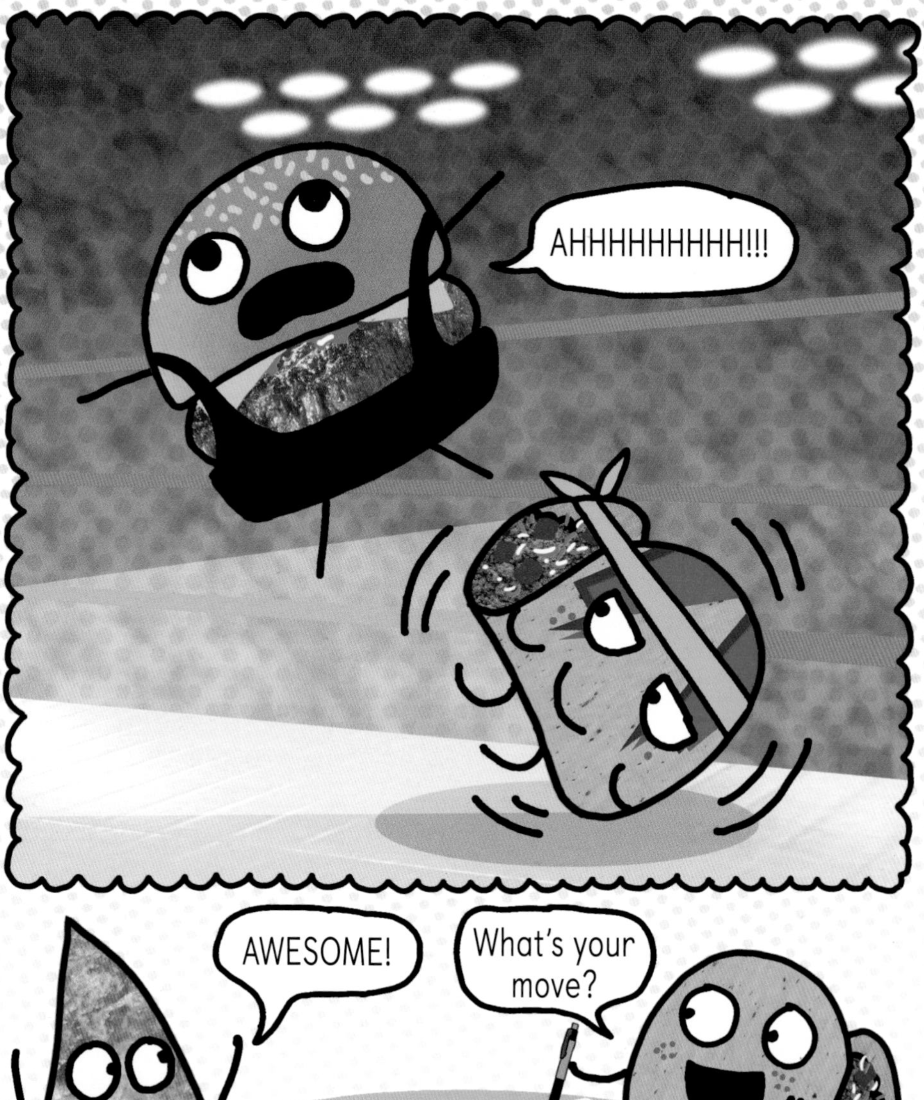
AHHHHHHHHH!!!

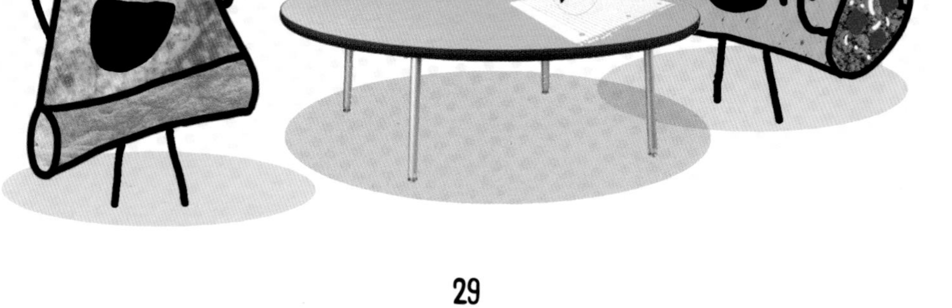
AWESOME!
What's your move?

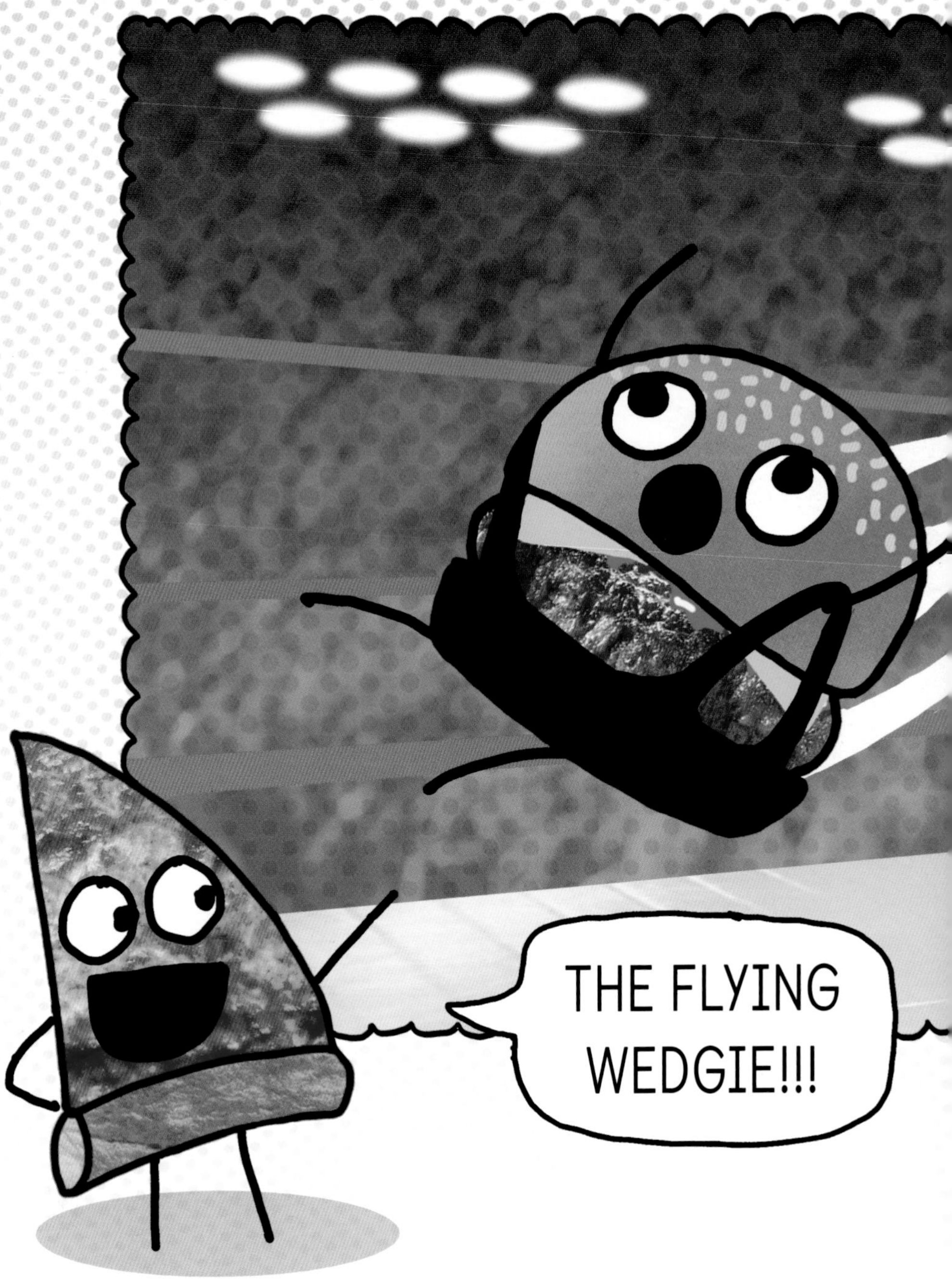
THE FLYING WEDGIE!!!

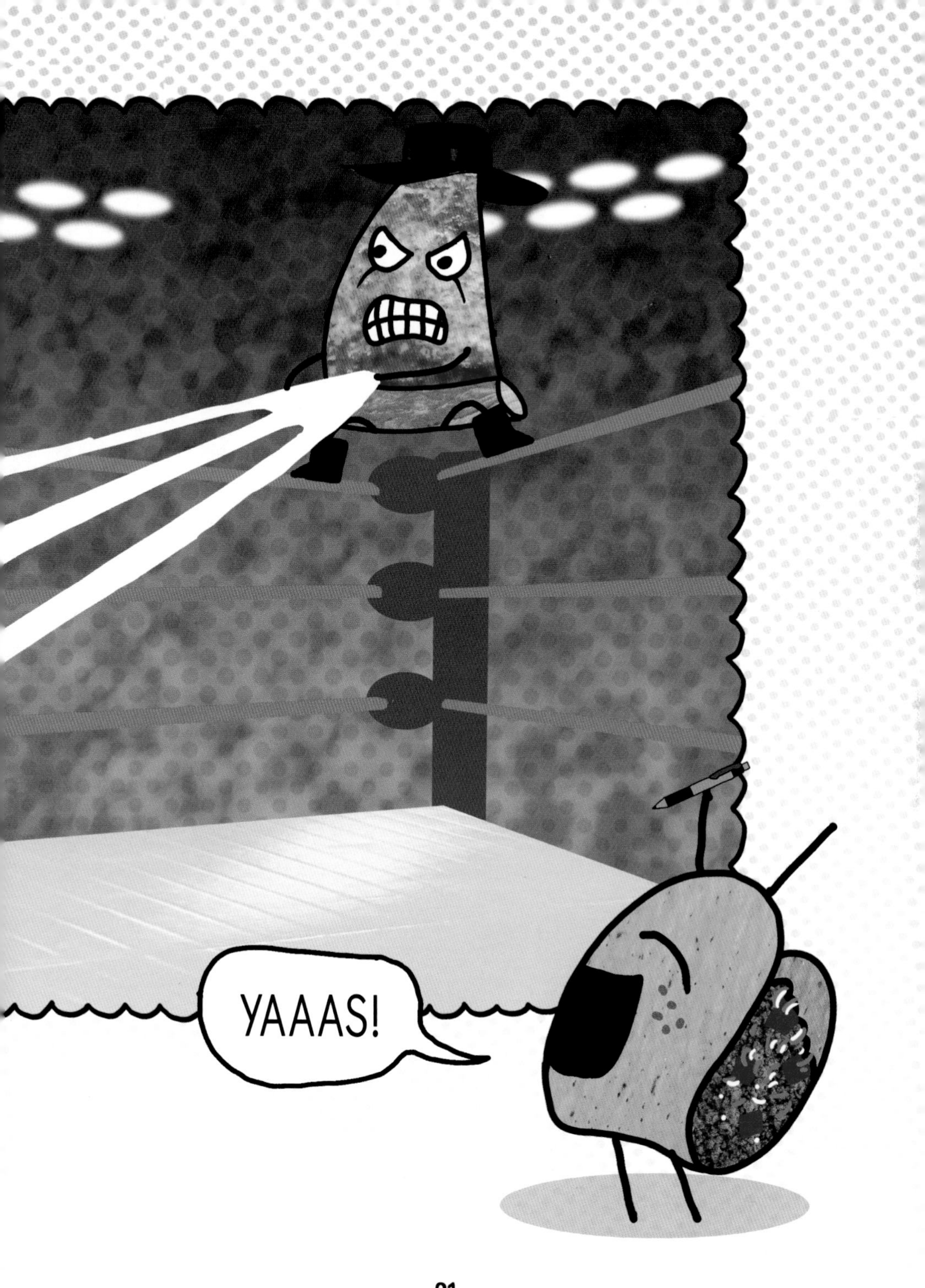
YAAAS!

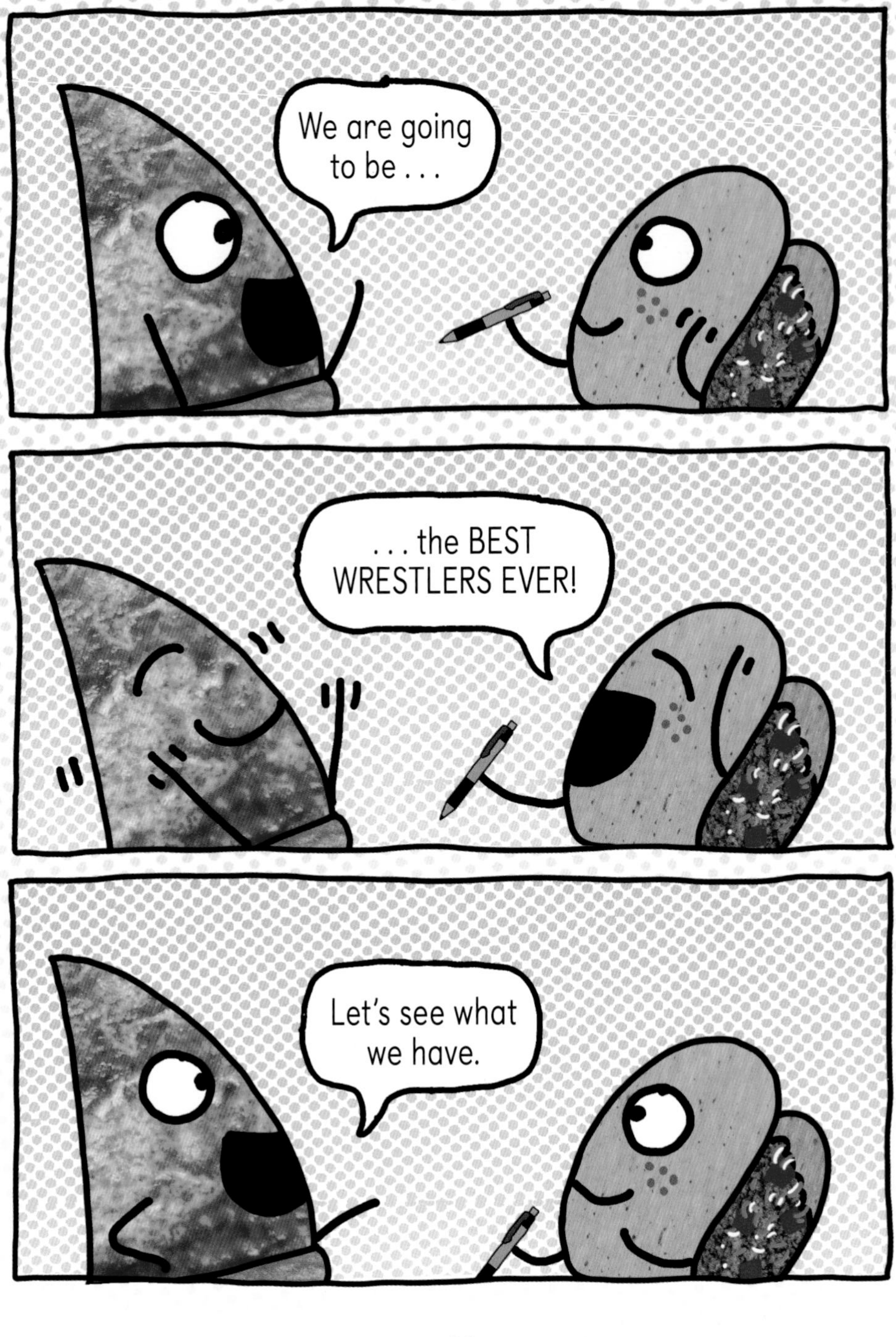
We are going to be . . .
. . . the BEST WRESTLERS EVER!
Let's see what we have.

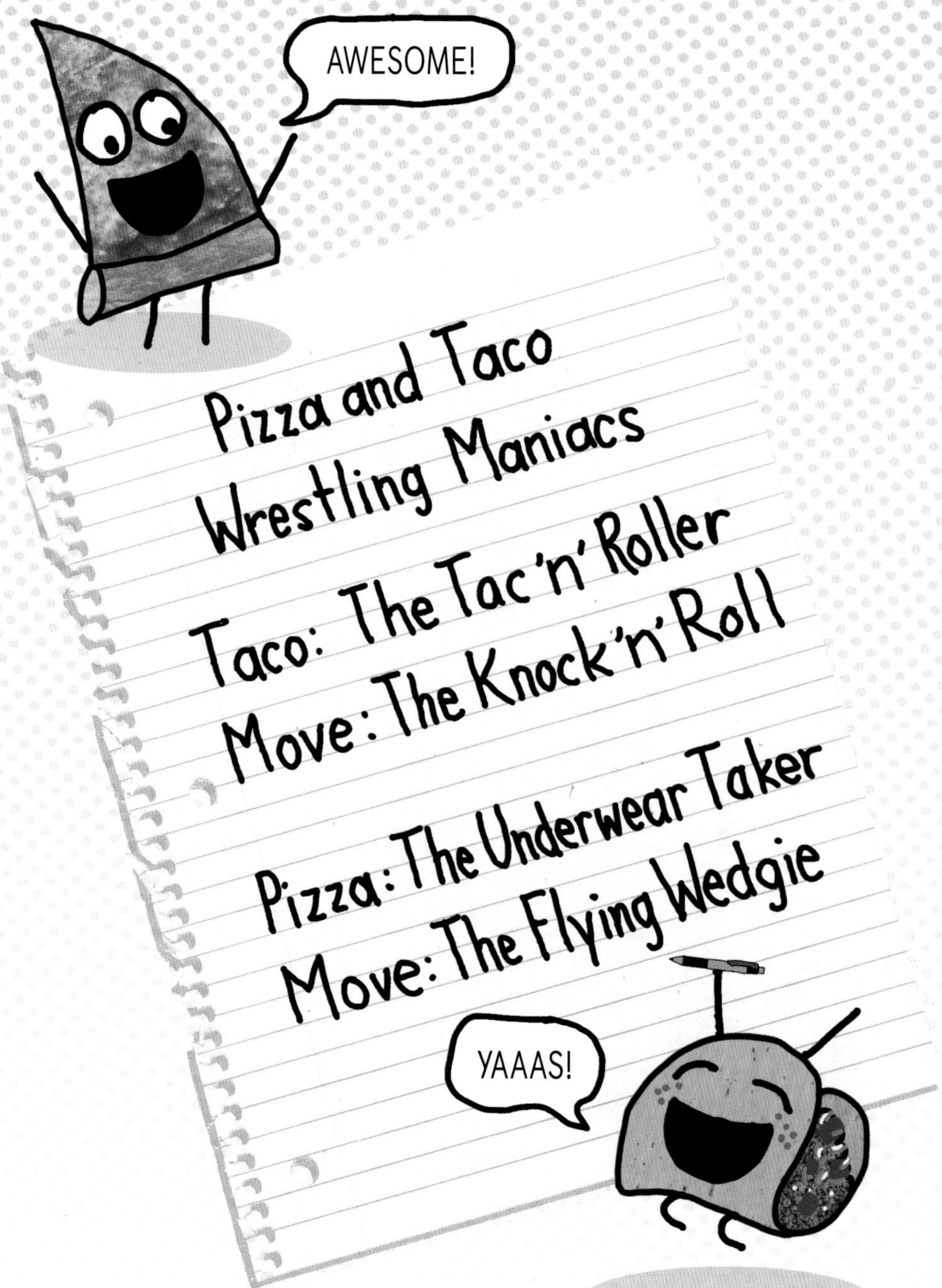
AWESOME!
Pizza and Taco
Wrestling Maniacs
Taco: The Tac'n' Roller
Move: The Knock'n' Roll
Pizza: The Underwear Taker
Move: The Flying Wedgie
YAAAS!

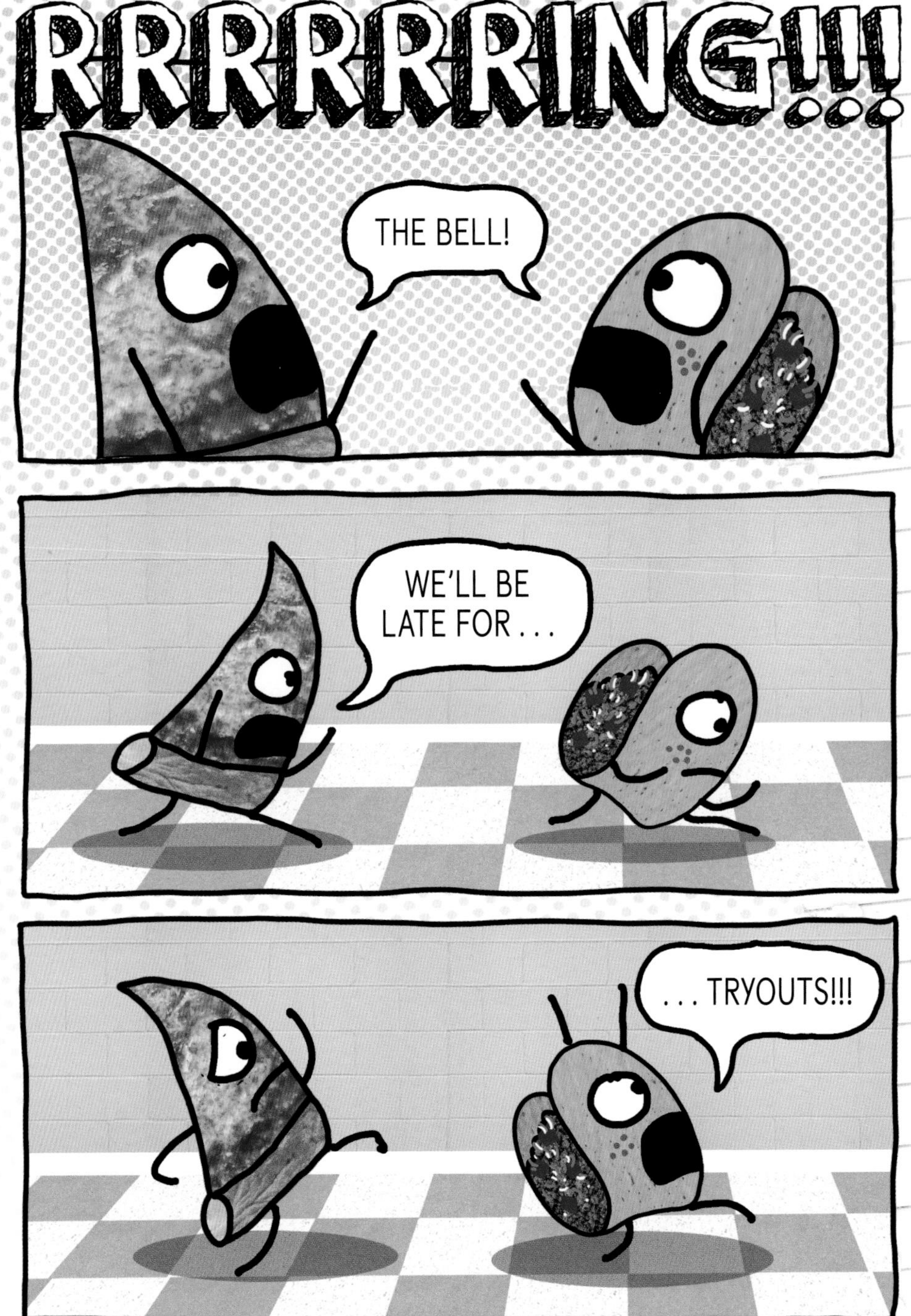
RRRRRRING!!!
THE BELL!
WE'LL BE LATE FOR . . .
. . . TRYOUTS!!!

Chapter 4
Tryouts

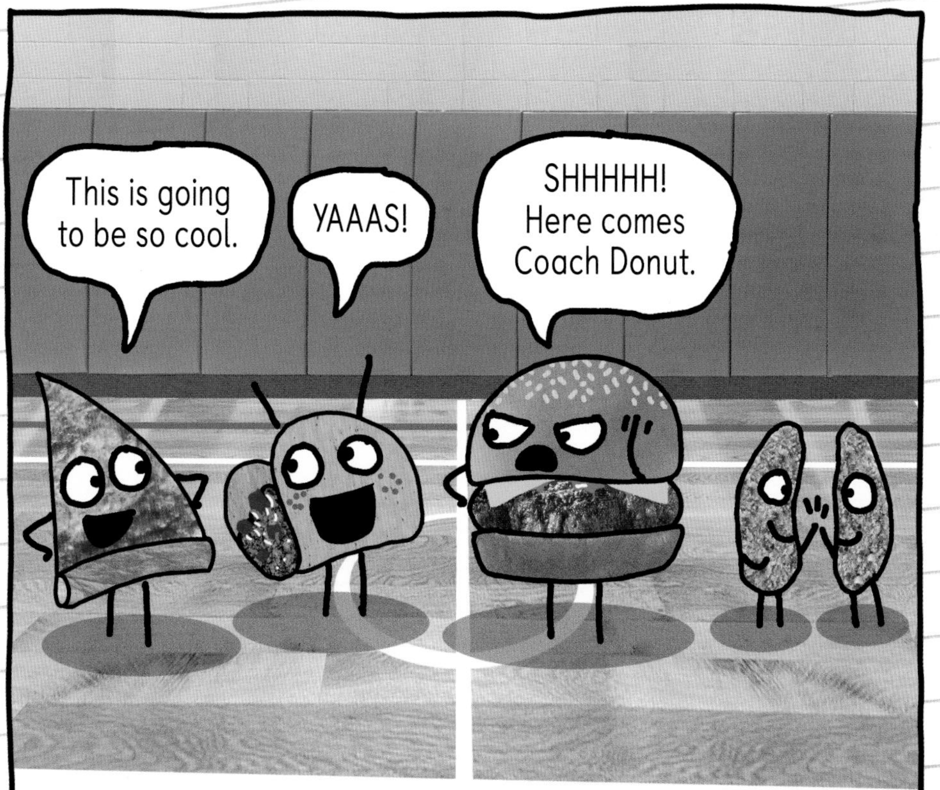
This is going to be so cool.
YAAAS!
SHHHHH! Here comes Coach Donut.

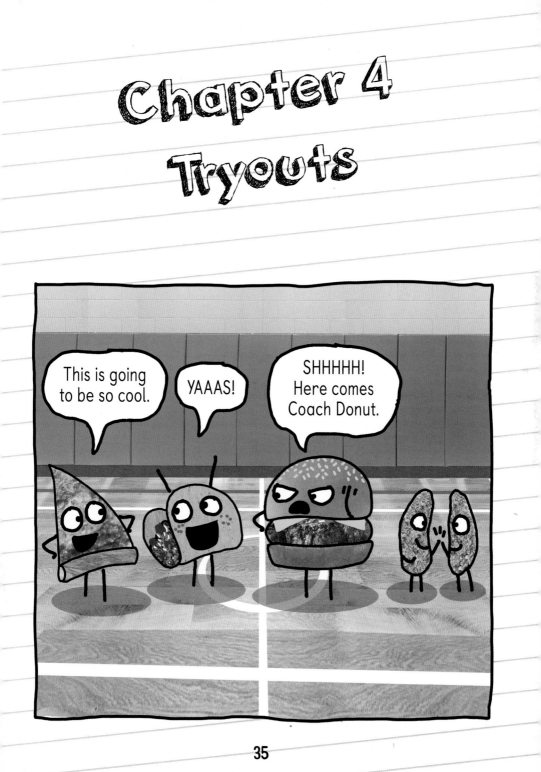

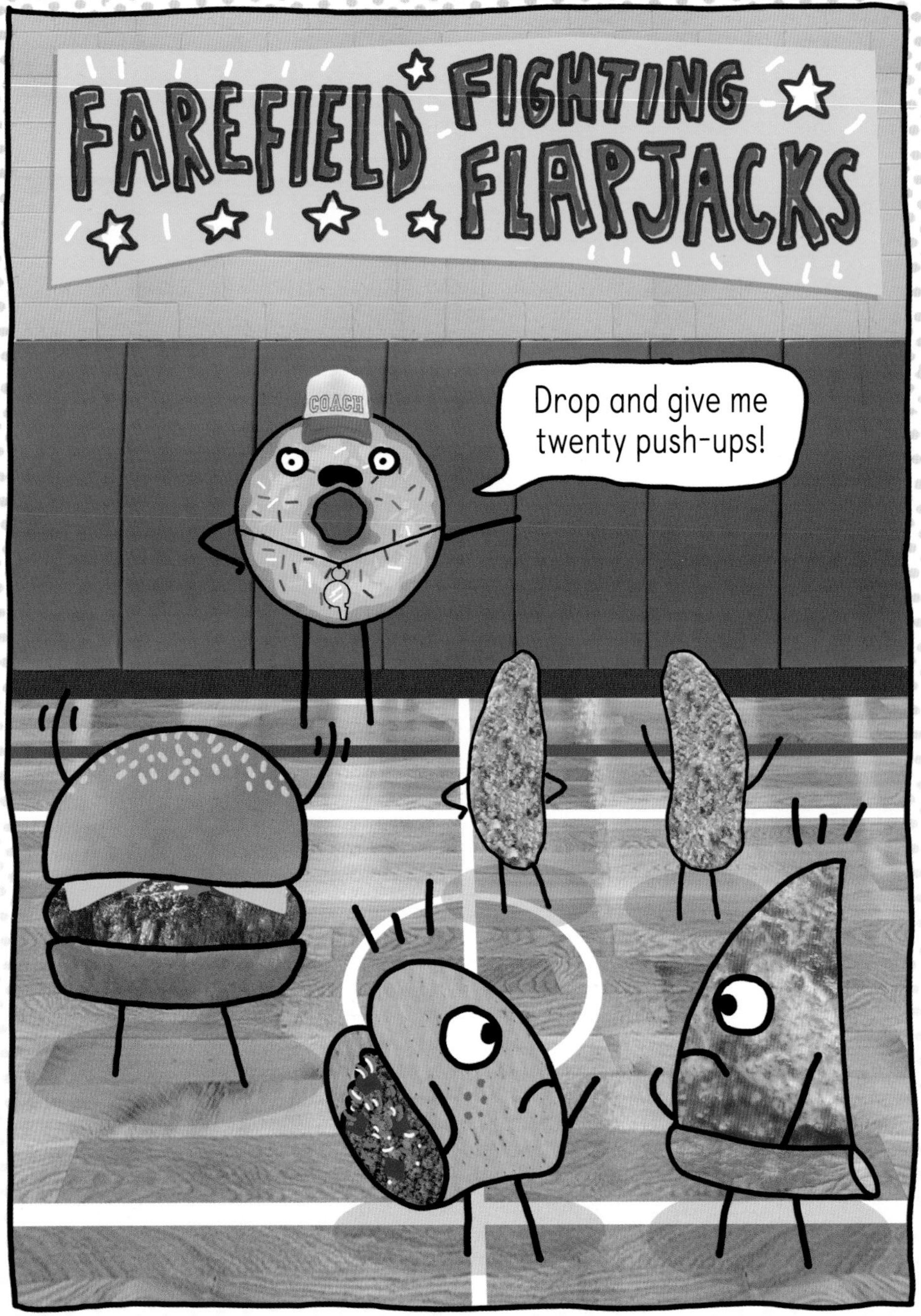
FAREFIELD FIGHTING FLAPJACKS
COACH
Drop and give me twenty push-ups!

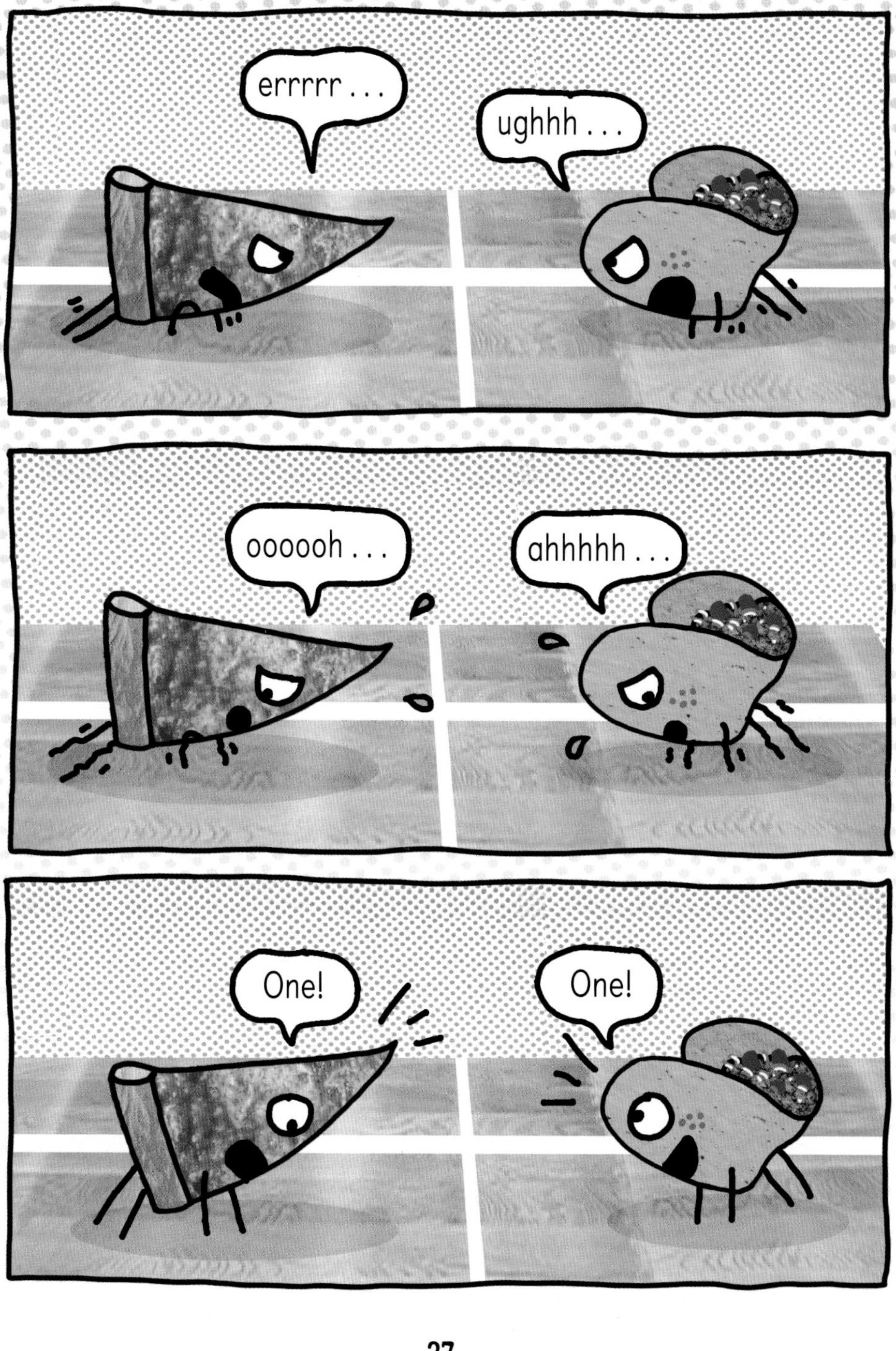
errrrr . . .
ughhh . . .
oooooh . . .
ahhhhh . . .
One!
One!

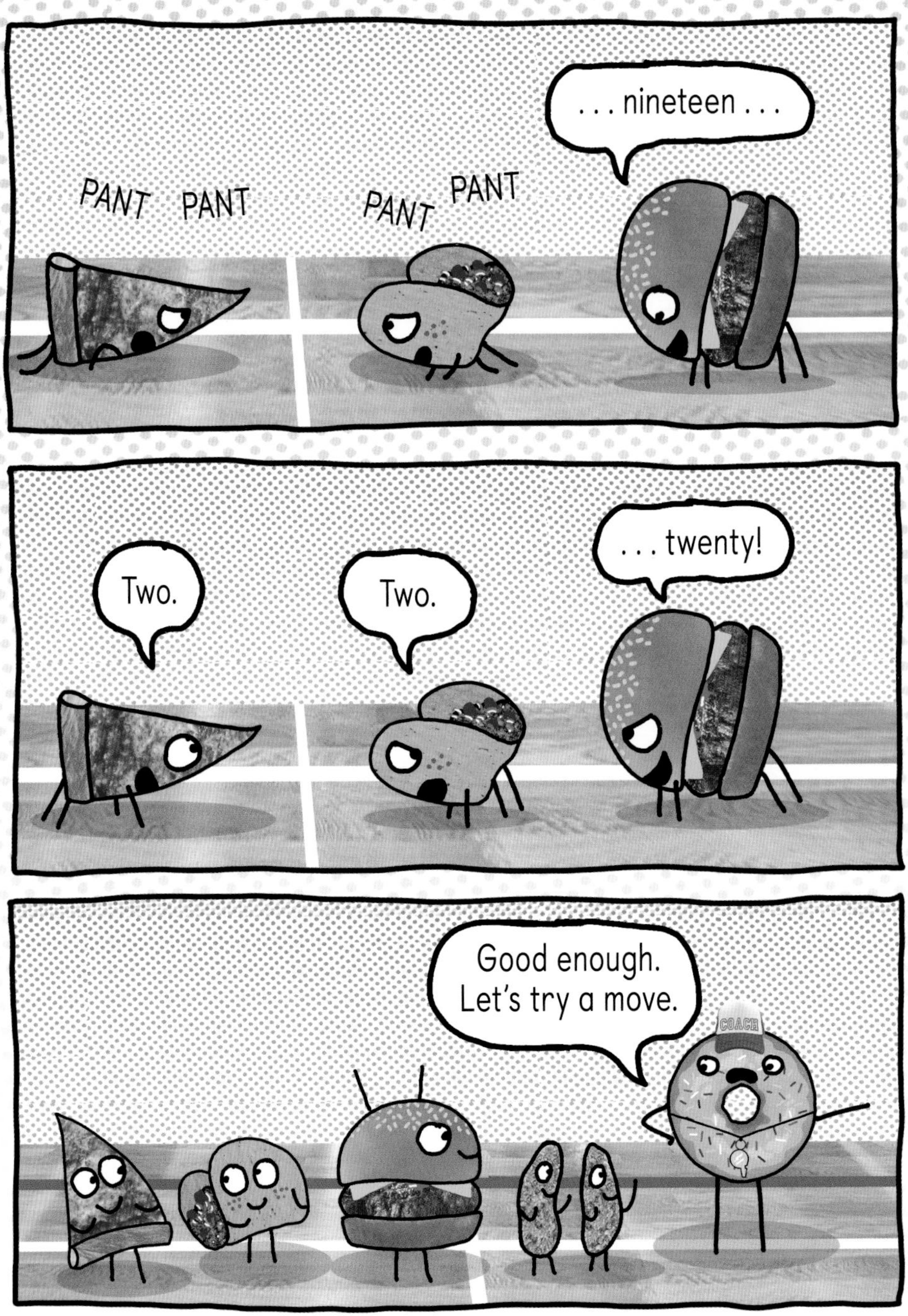
PANT PANT
PANT PANT
. . . nineteen . . .
Two.
Two.
. . . twenty!
Good enough.
Let's try a move.
COACH

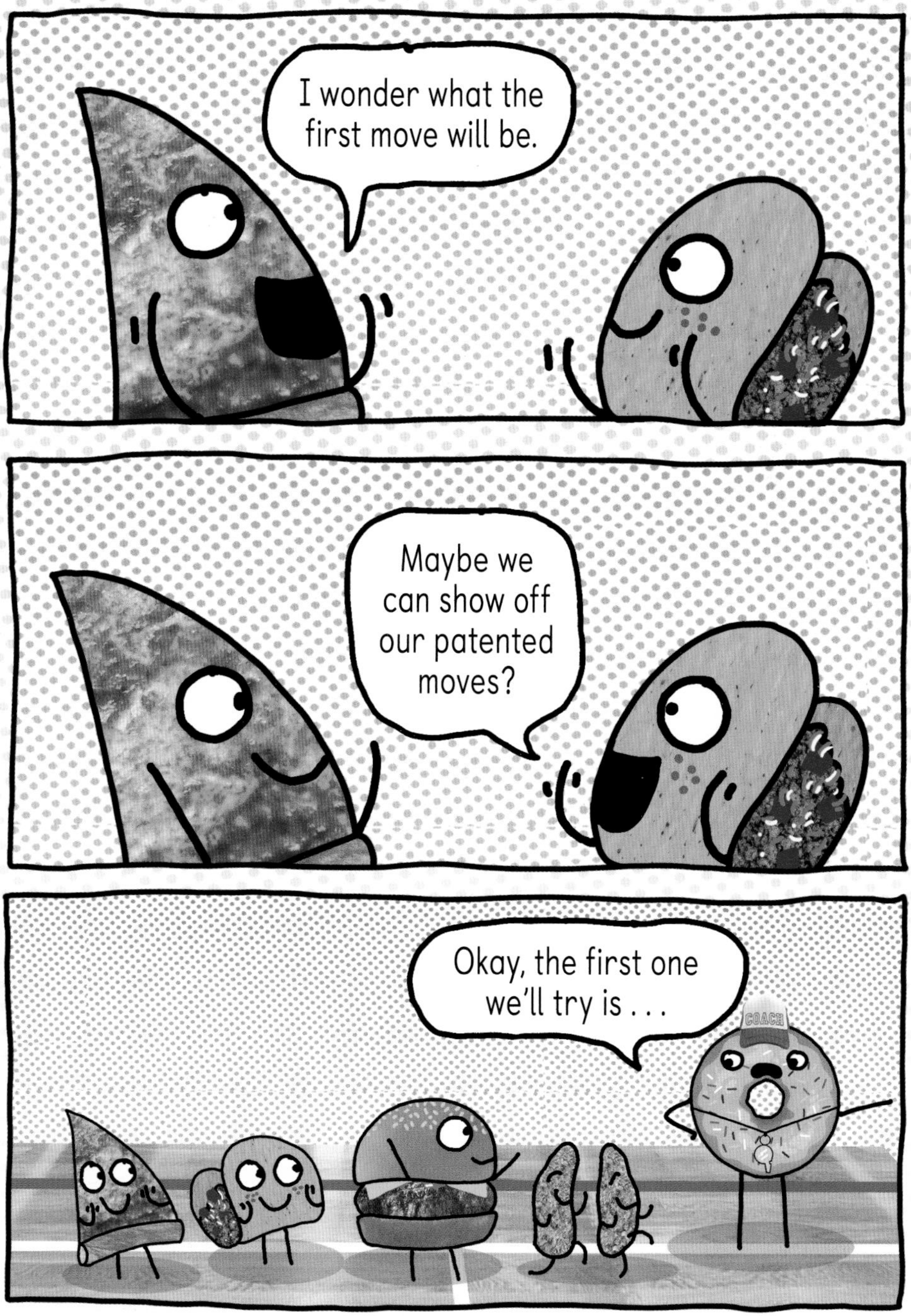
I wonder what the first move will be.
Maybe we can show off our patented moves?
Okay, the first one we'll try is . . .
COACH

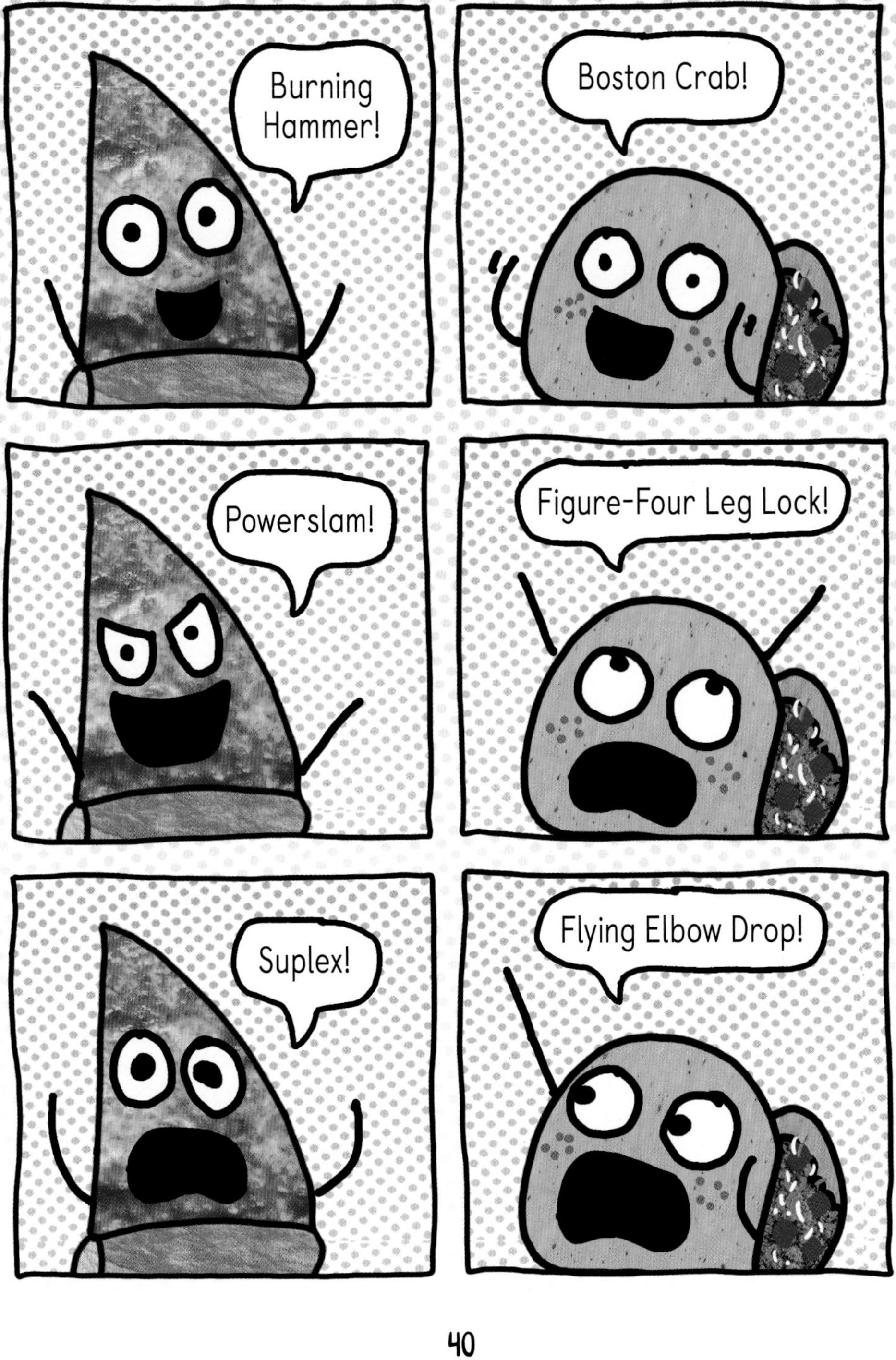

Burning Hammer!
Boston Crab!
Powerslam!
Figure-Four Leg Lock!
Suplex!
Flying Elbow Drop!

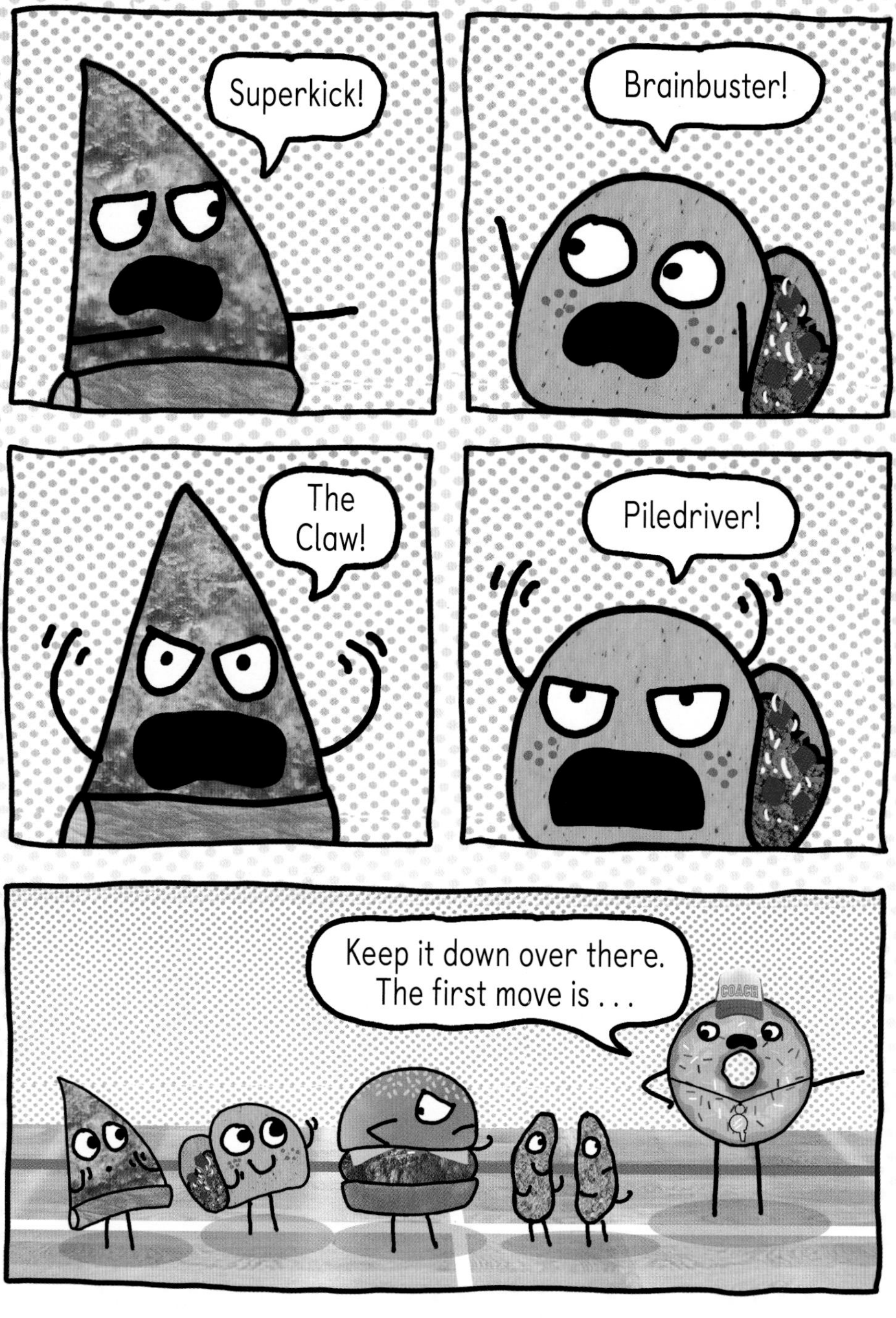
Superkick!
Brainbuster!
The Claw!
Piledriver!
Keep it down over there. The first move is . . .
COACH

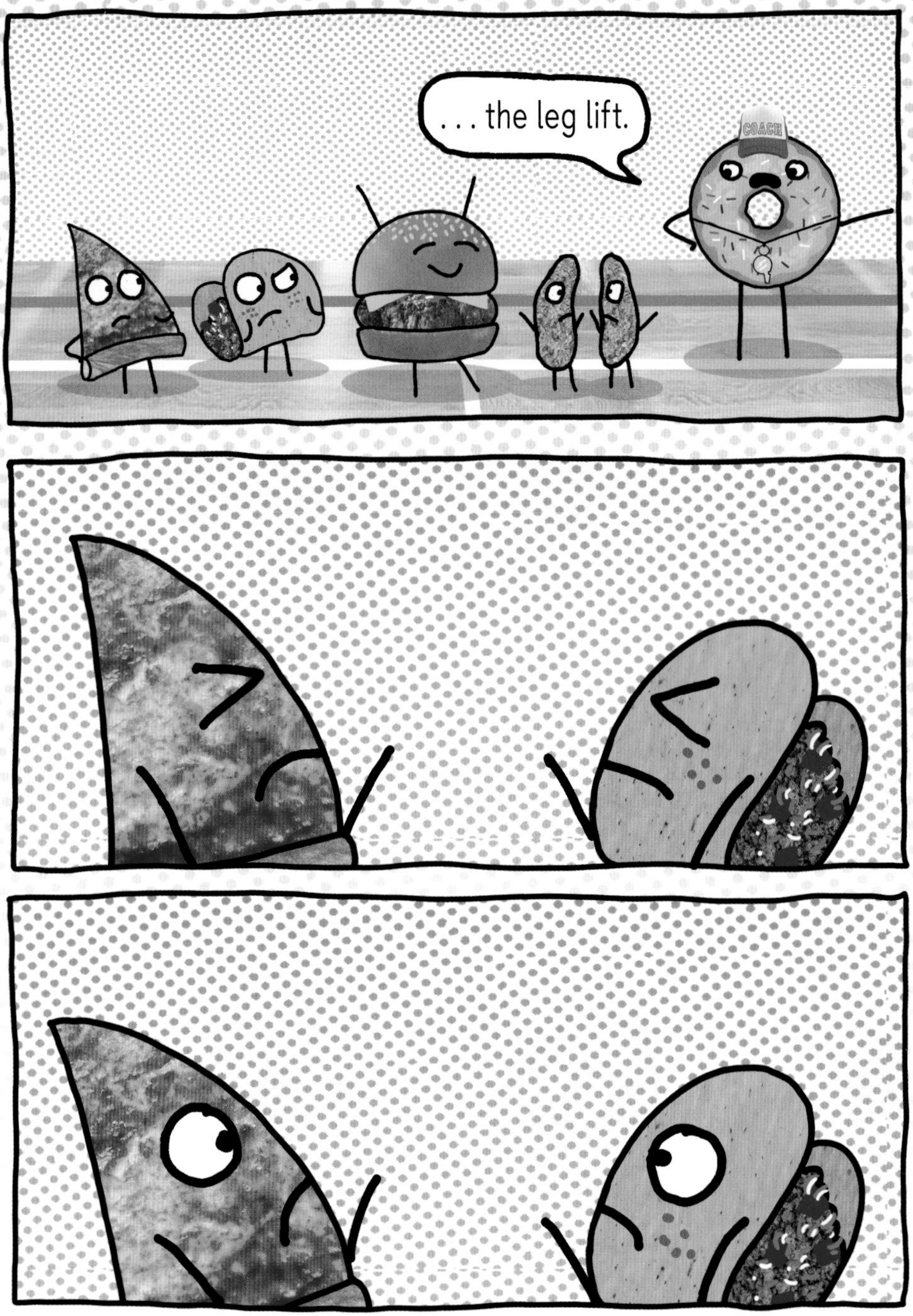
. . . the leg lift.
COACH

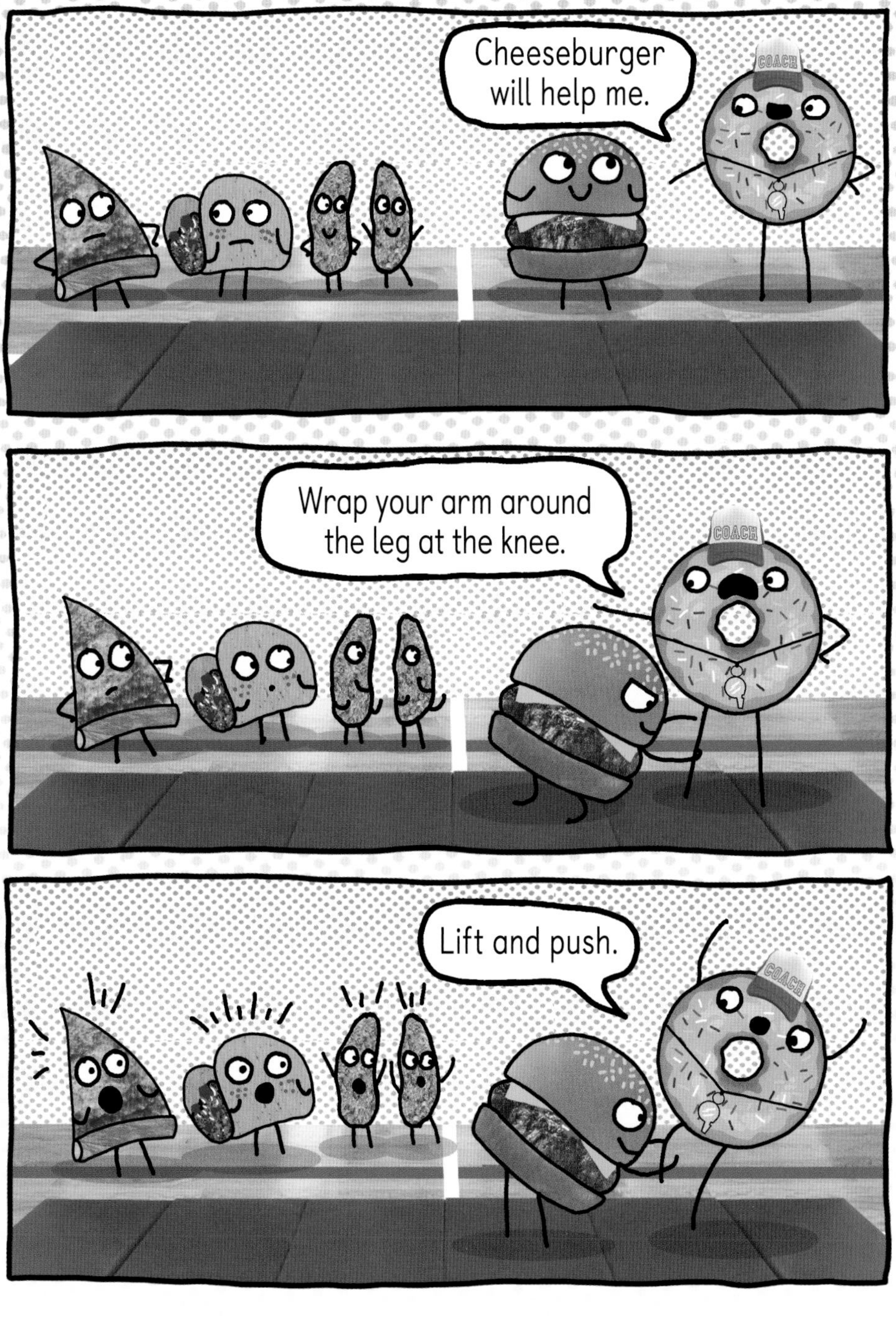
Cheeseburger will help me.
COACH
COACH
Wrap your arm around the leg at the knee.
Lift and push.
COACH

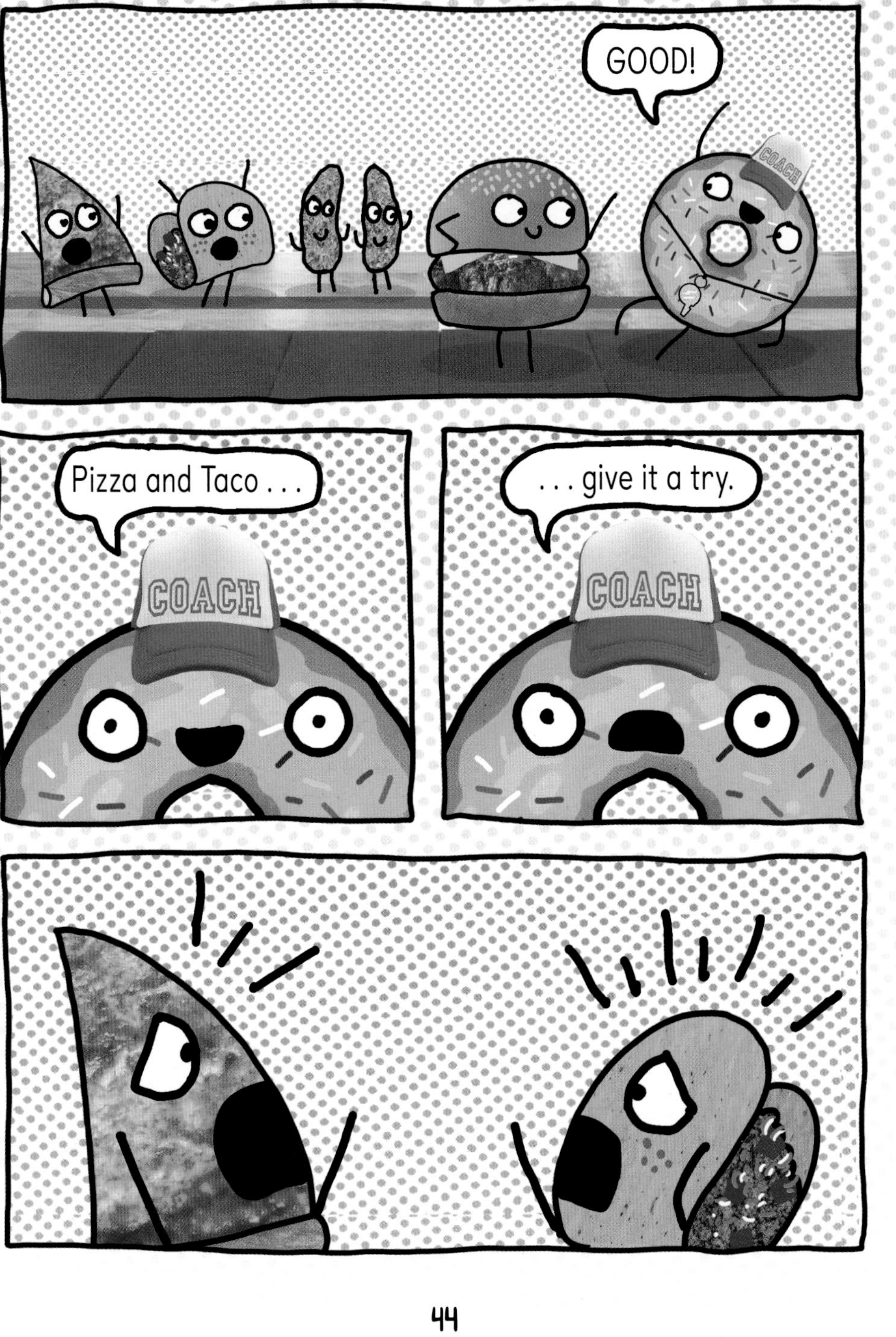
GOOD!
COACH
Pizza and Taco . . .
COACH
. . . give it a try.
COACH

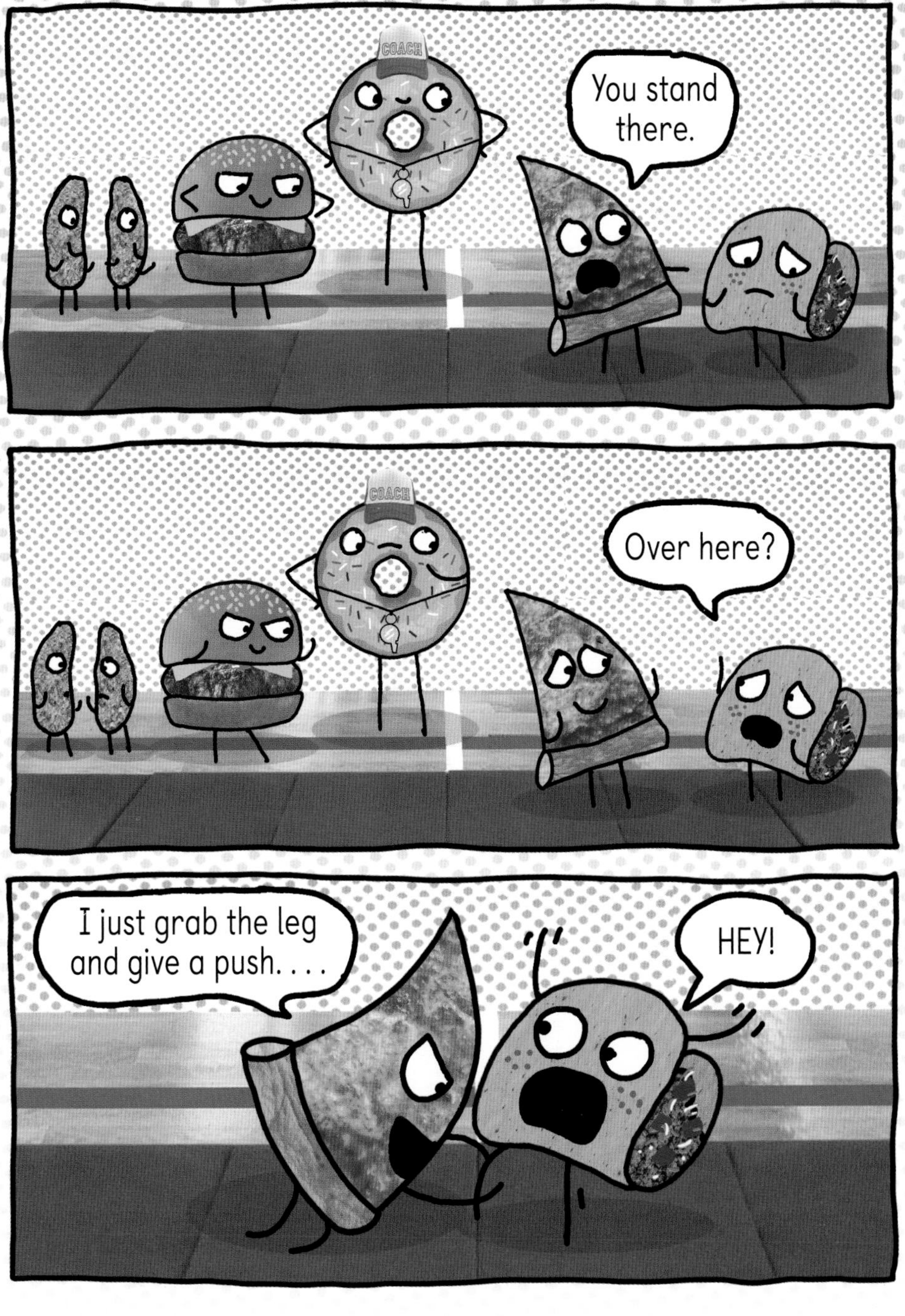
COACH
You stand there.
COACH
Over here?
I just grab the leg and give a push. . . .
HEY!

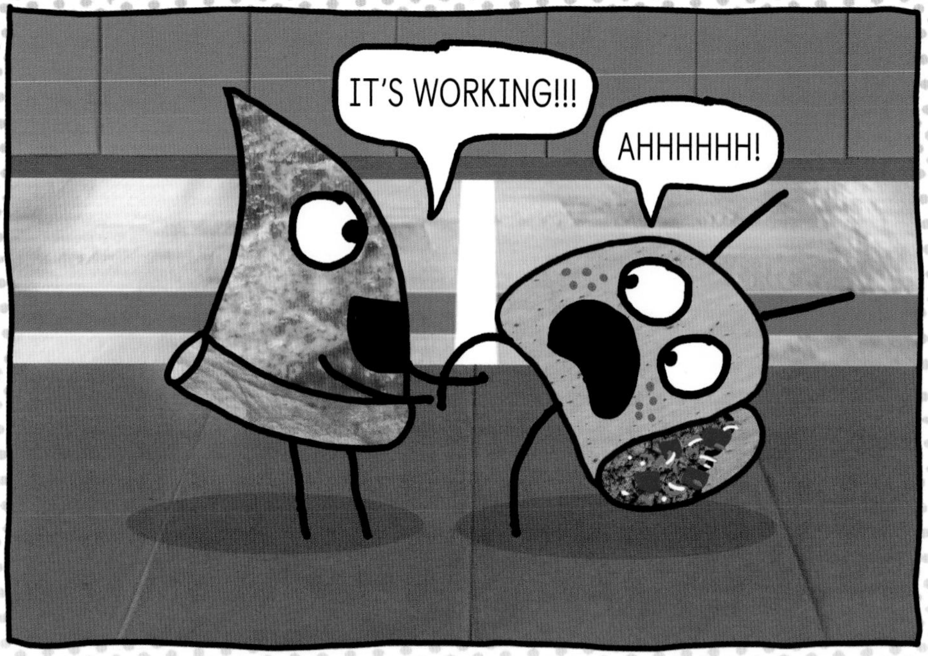
IT'S WORKING!!!
AHHHHHH!

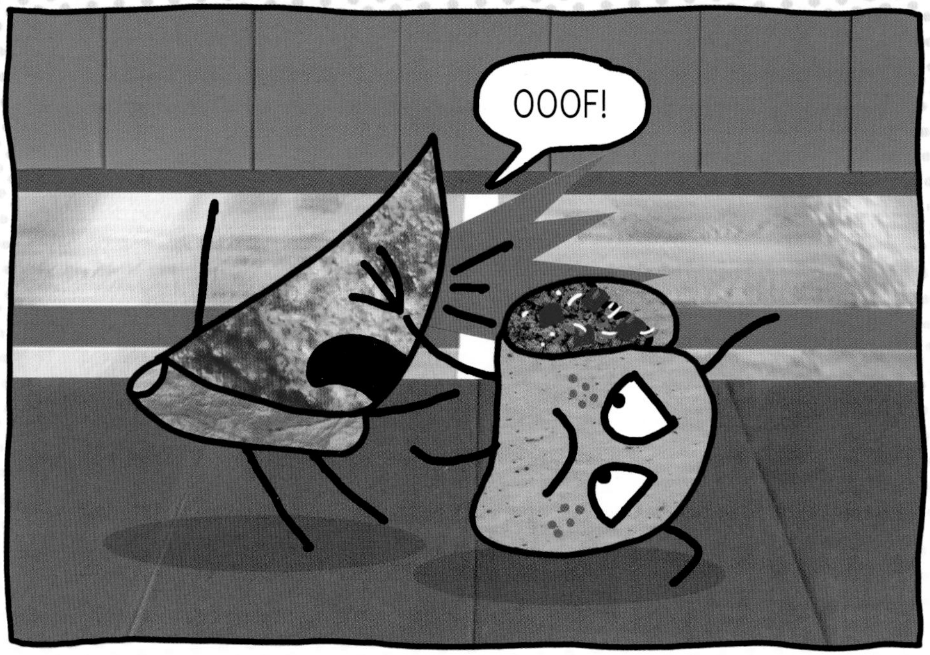
OOOF!

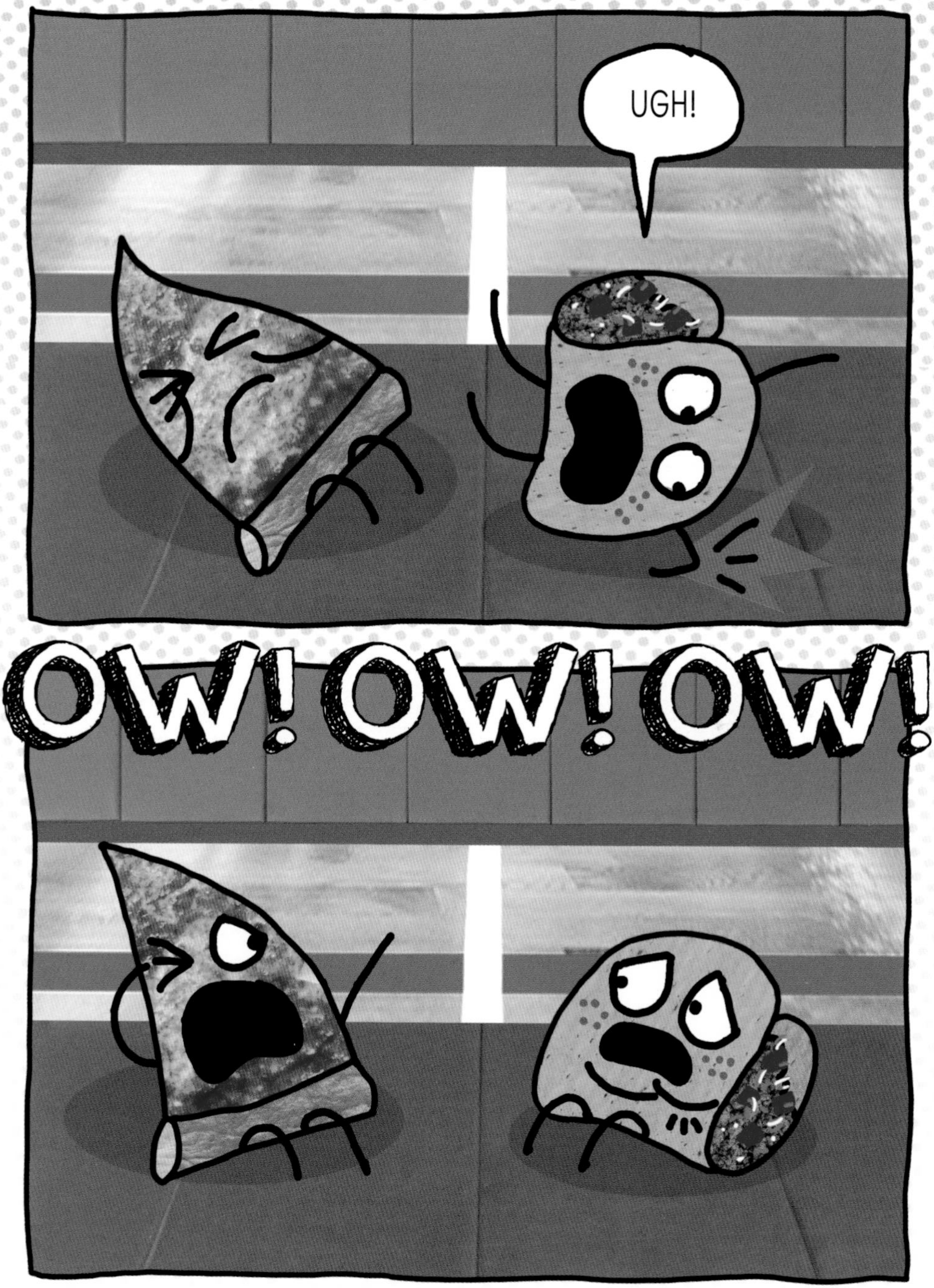
UGH!
OW! OW! OW!

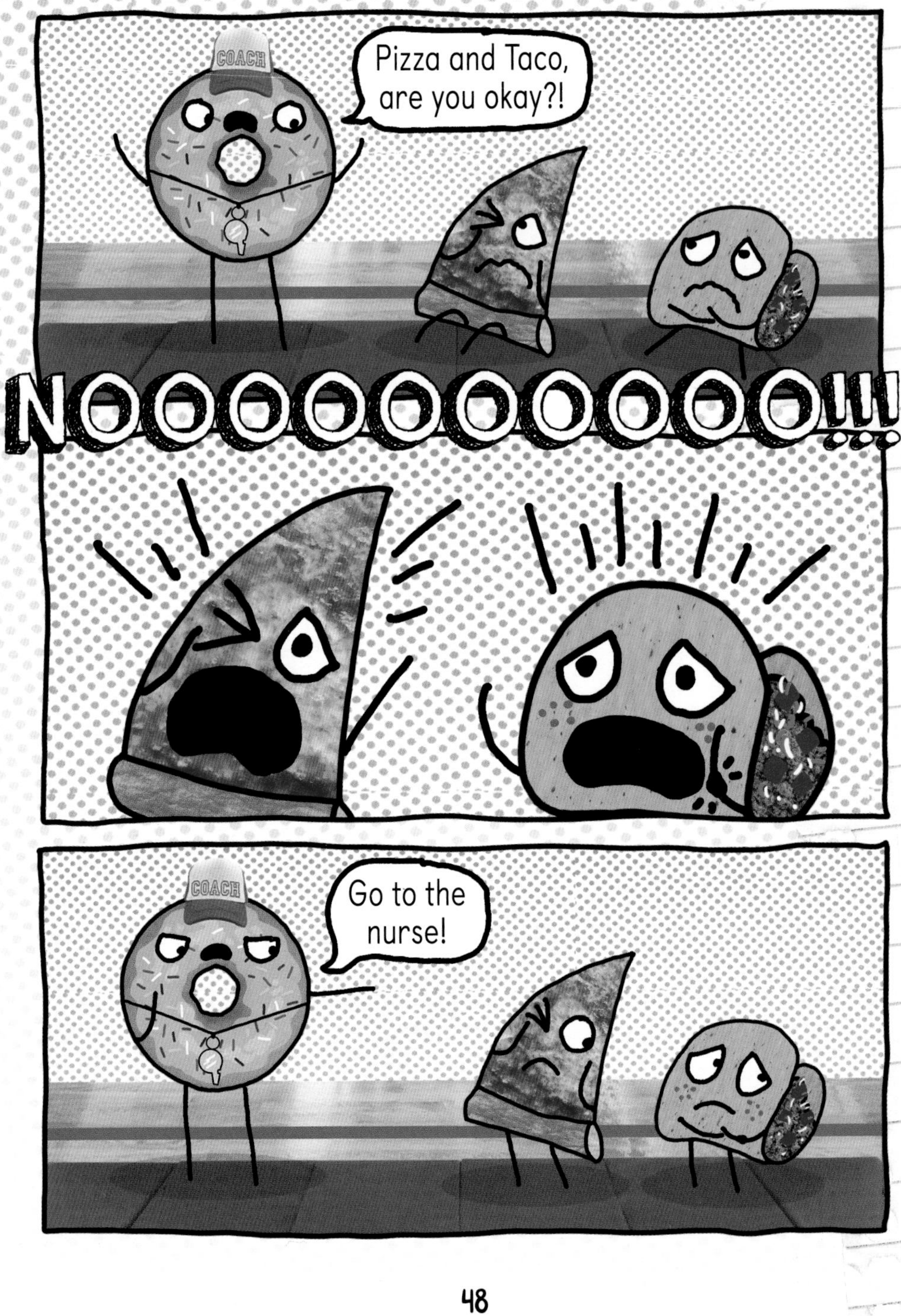
COACH
Pizza and Taco, are you okay?!
NOOOOOOOOOOOO!!!!
COACH
Go to the nurse!

Chapter 5
Clubs

FIRST AID
That was so not awesome.
ICE PACK
ICE PACK

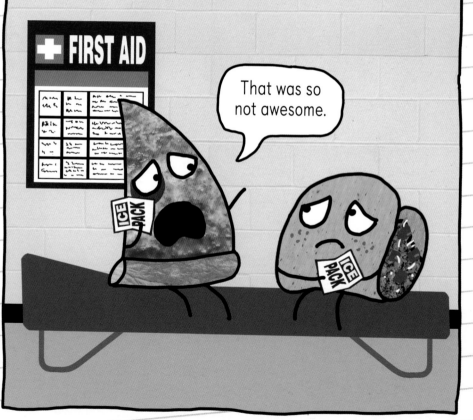

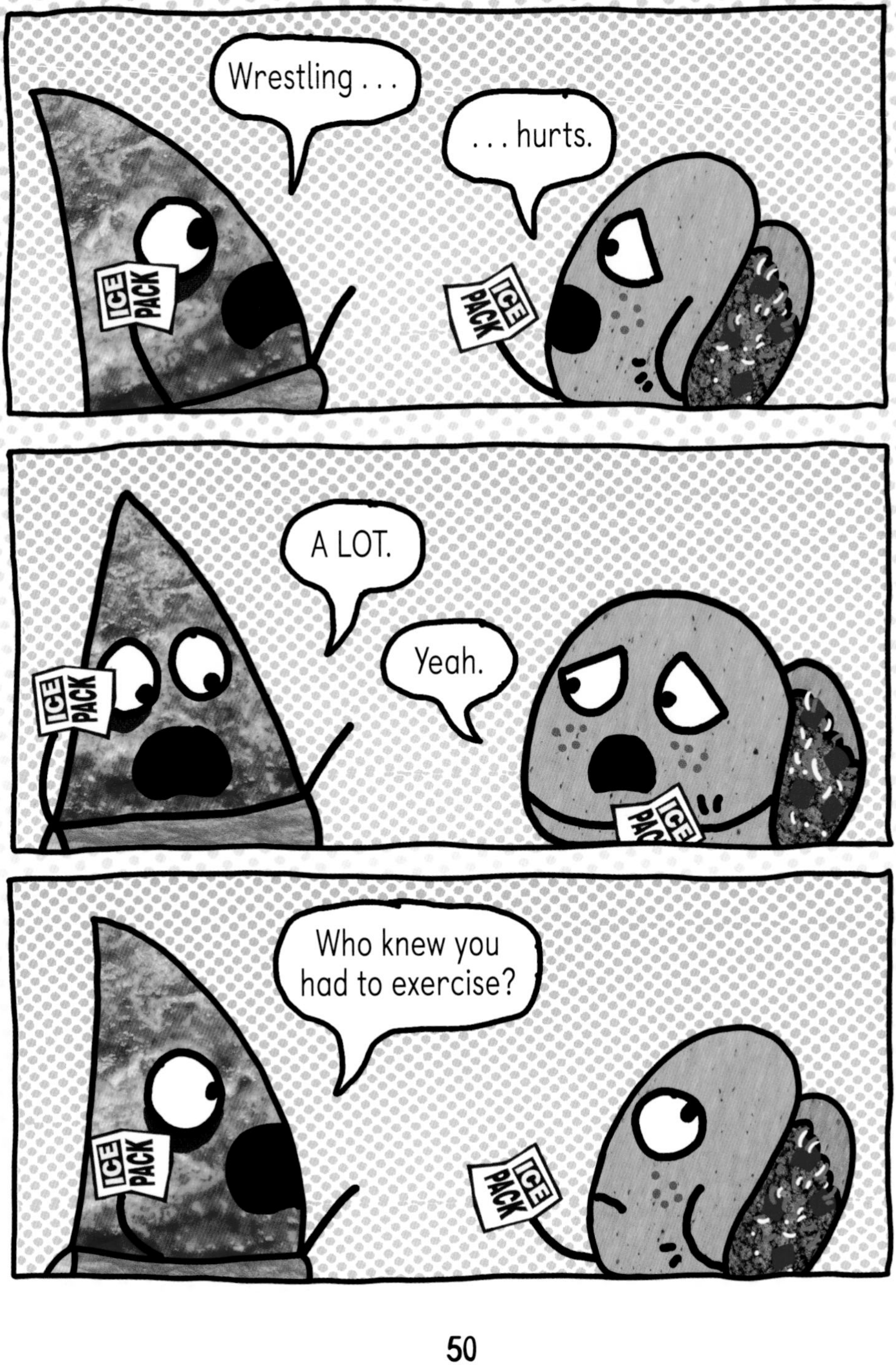
Wrestling . . .
. . . hurts.
ICE PACK
ICE PACK
A LOT.
Yeah.
ICE PACK
Who knew you had to exercise?
ICE PACK
ICE PACK

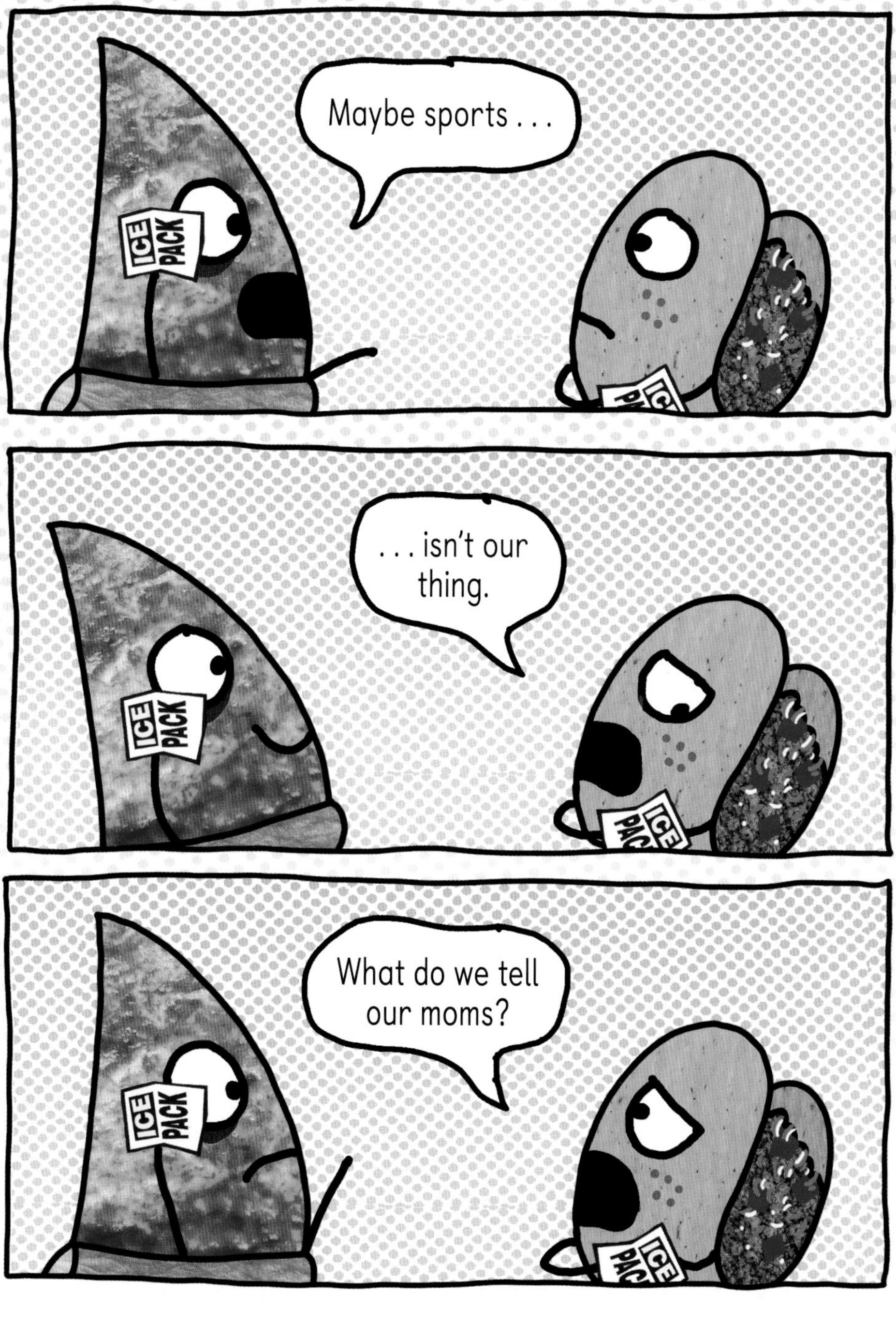
Maybe sports . . .
ICE PACK
. . . isn't our thing.
What do we tell our moms?

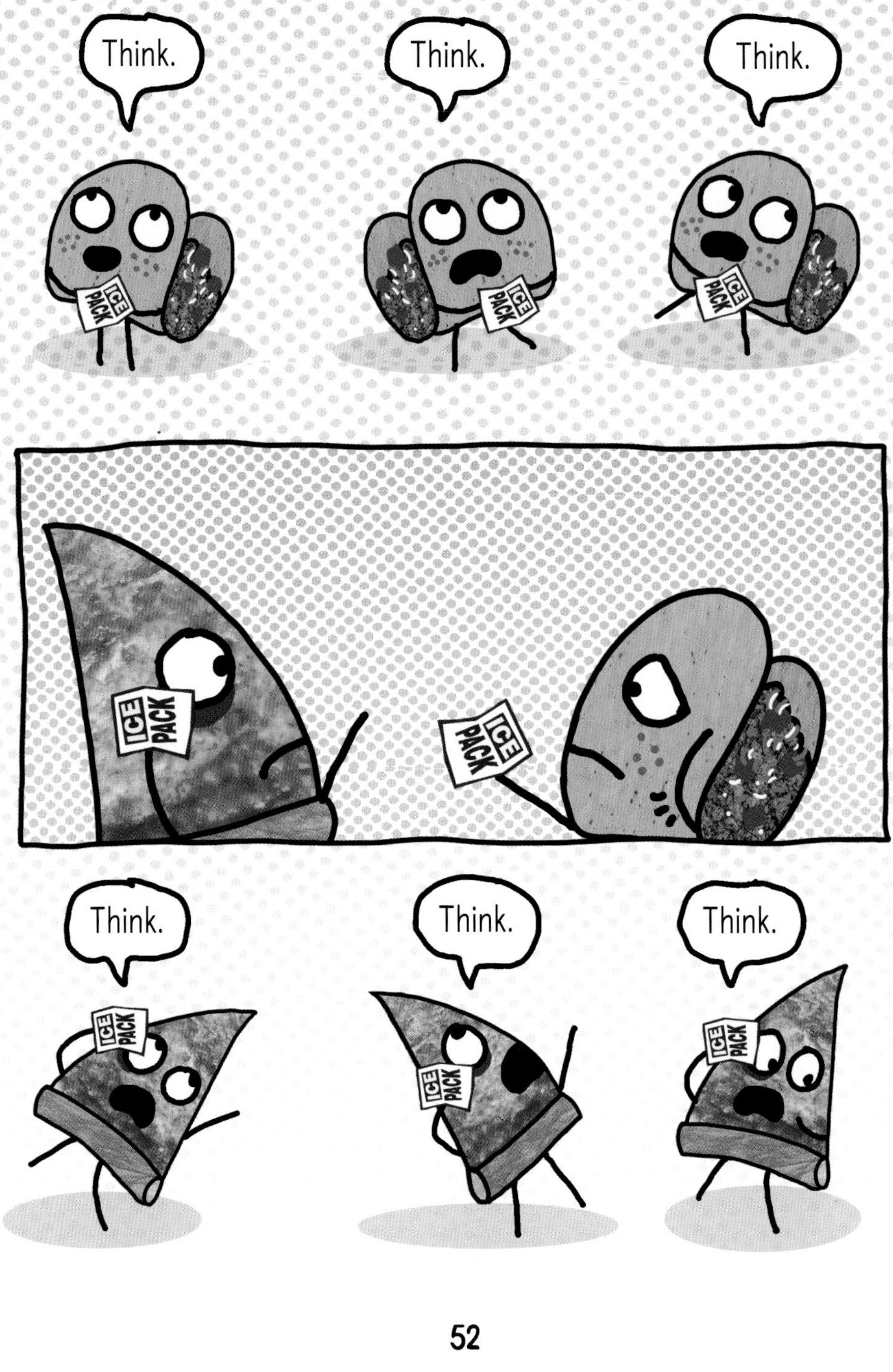
Think.
Think.
Think.
ICE PACK
ICE PACK
ICE PACK
ICE PACK
ICE PACK
Think.
Think.
Think.
ICE PACK
ICE PACK
ICE PACK

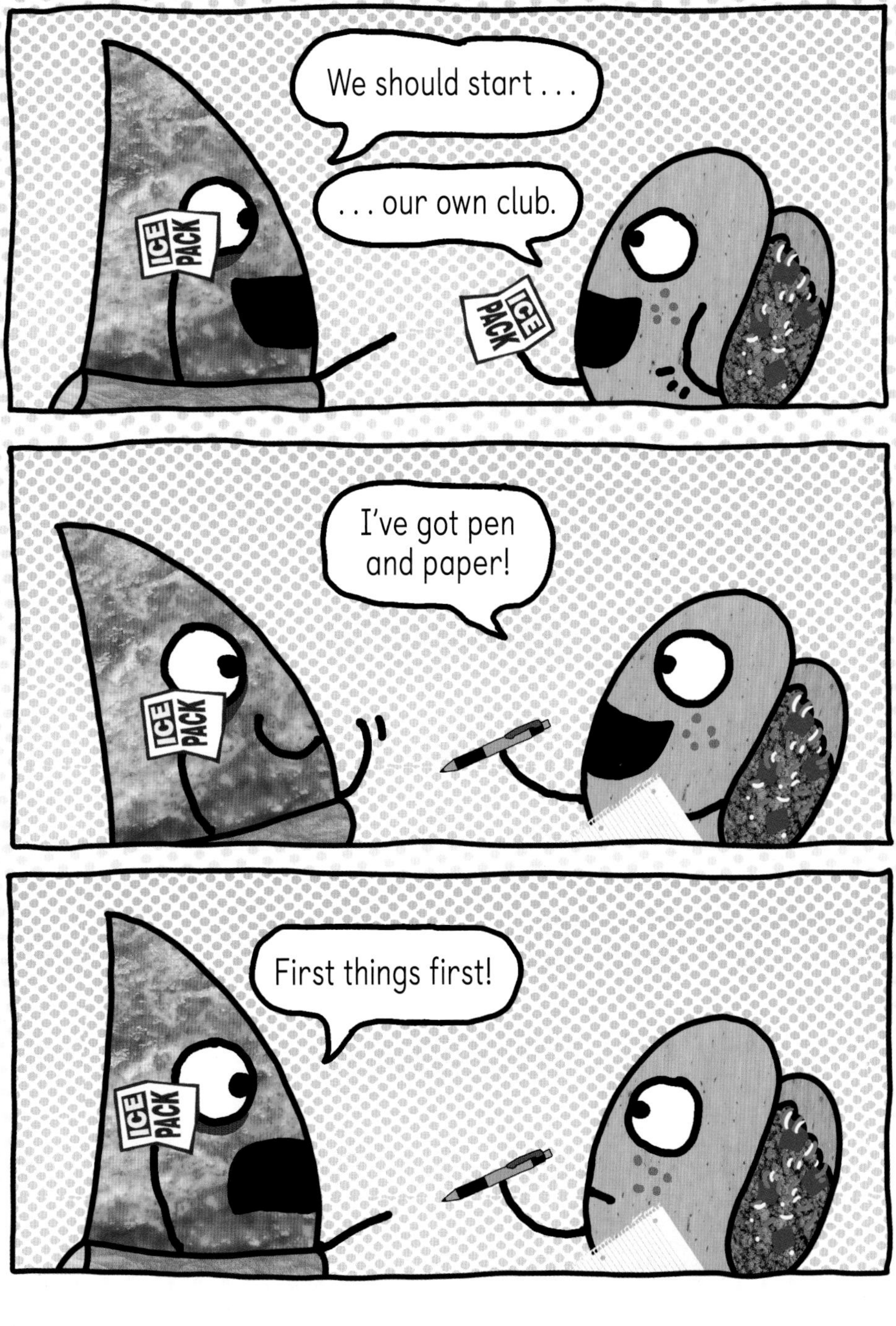
We should start . . .
. . . our own club.
ICE PACK
ICE PACK
I've got pen and paper!
ICE PACK
First things first!
ICE PACK

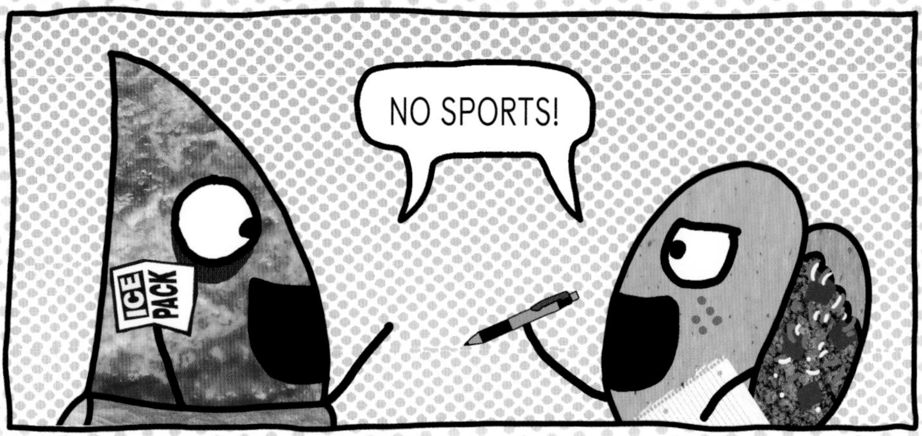
NO SPORTS!
ICE PACK

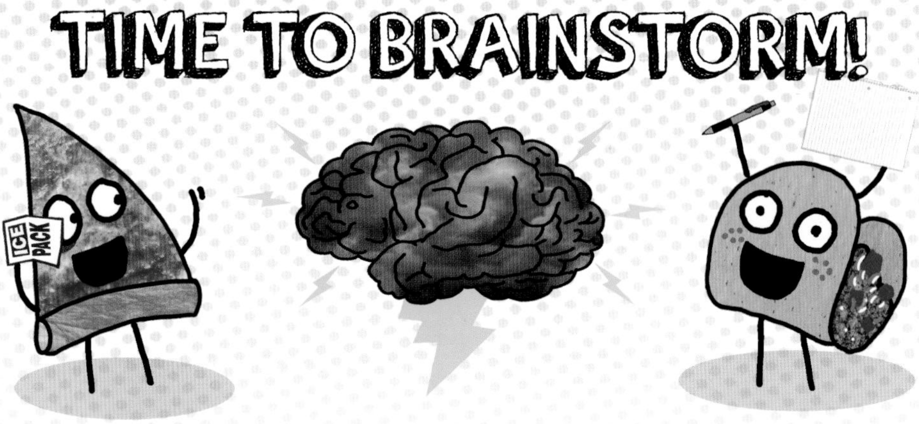
TIME TO BRAINSTORM!
ICE PACK

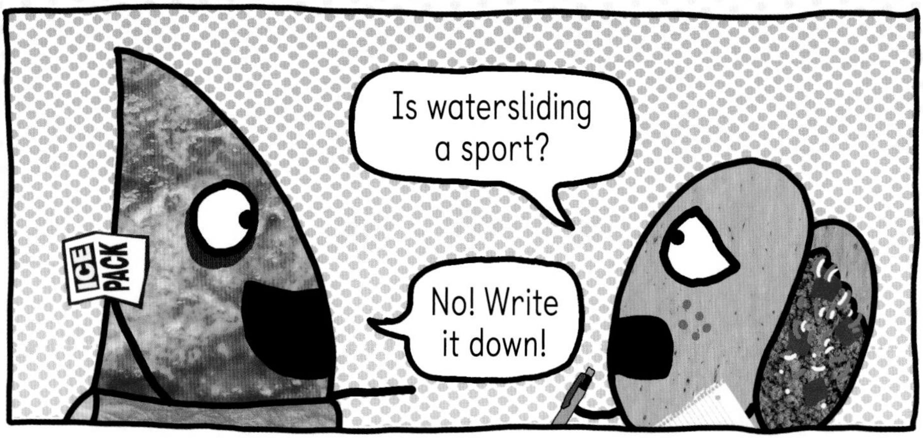
Is watersliding a sport?
No! Write it down!
ICE PACK

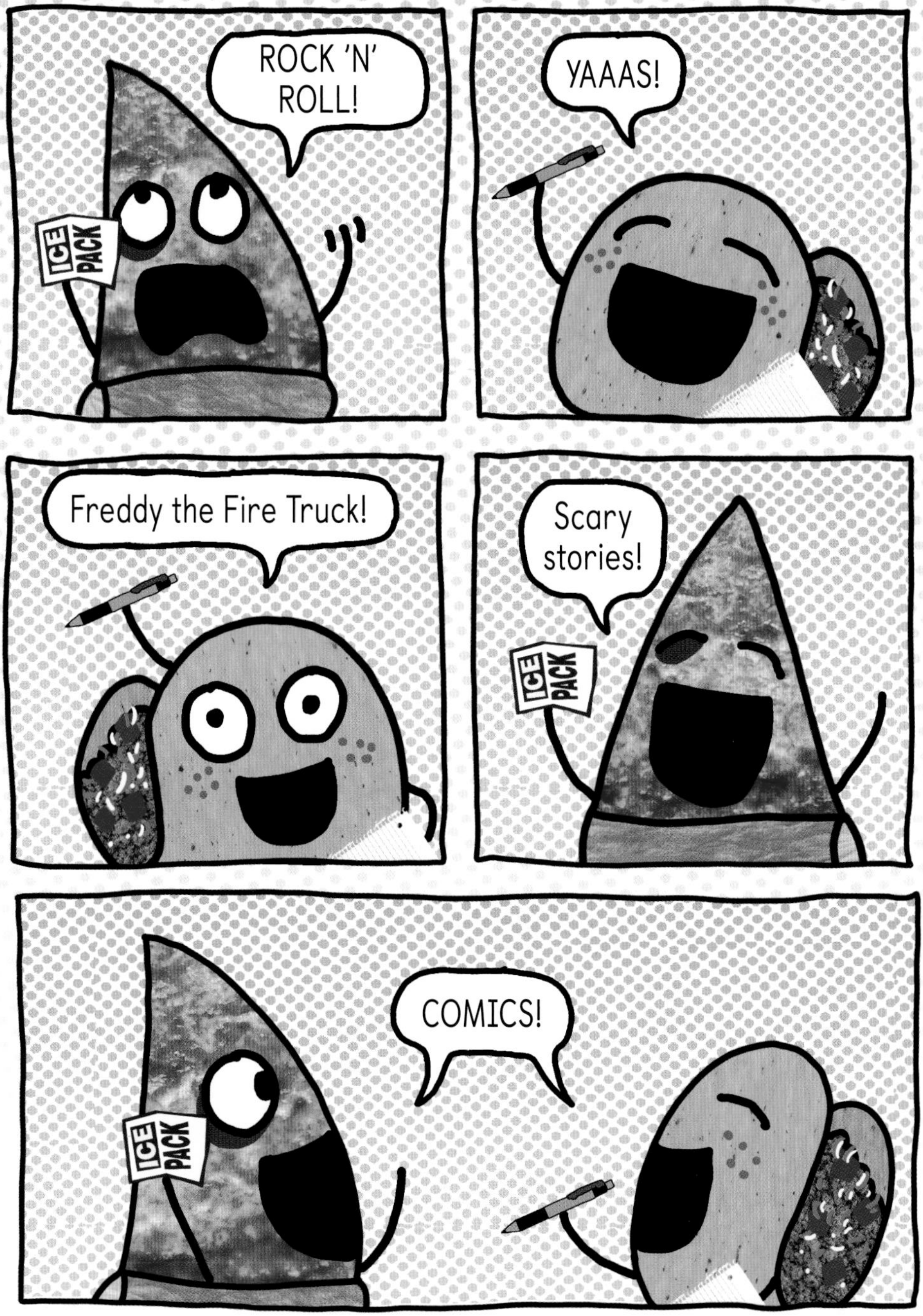
ROCK 'N' ROLL!
YAAAS!
Freddy the Fire Truck!
Scary stories!
ICE PACK
COMICS!

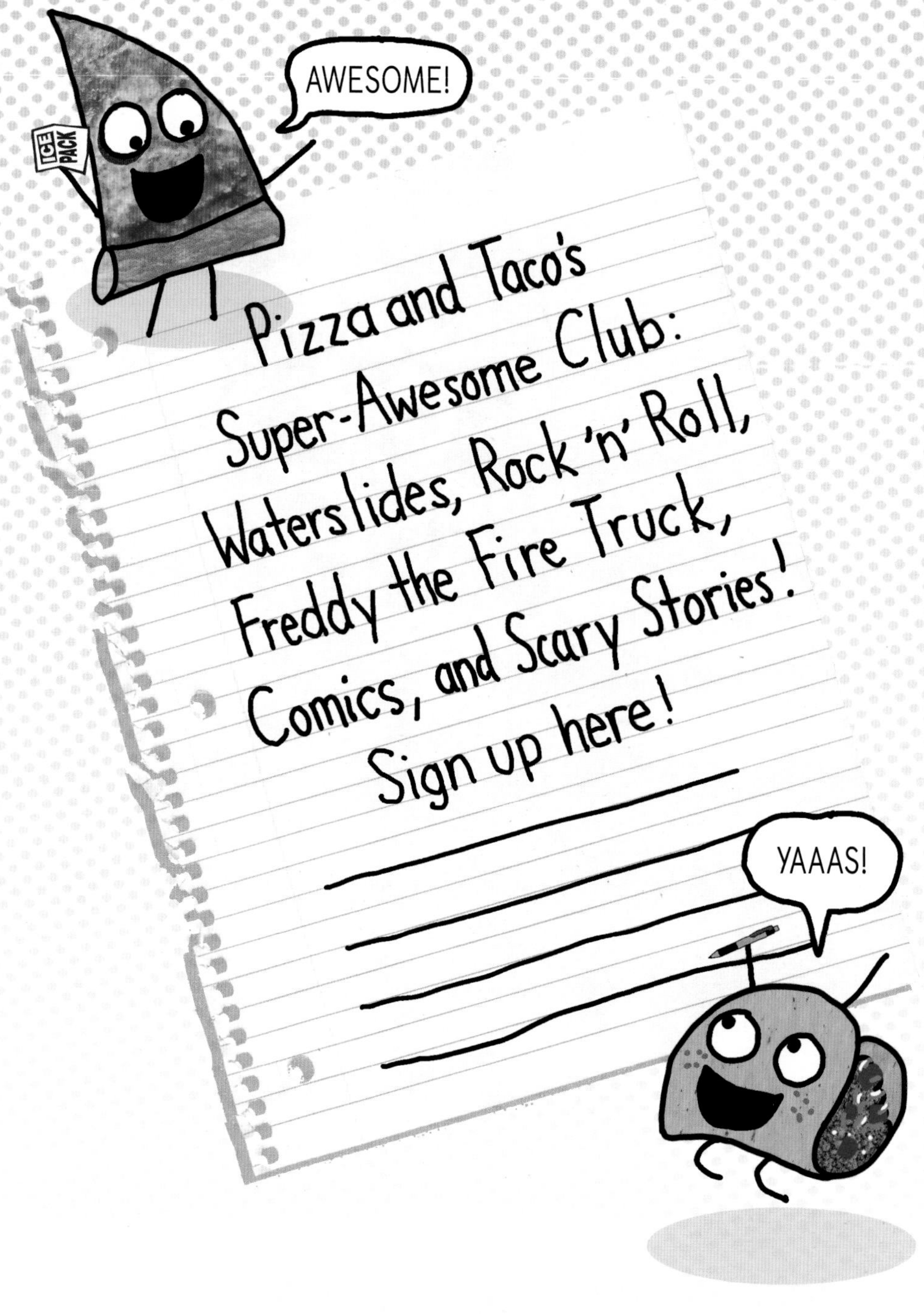
AWESOME!
ICE PACK
Pizza and Taco's
Super-Awesome Club:
Waterslides, Rock 'n' Roll,
Freddy the Fire Truck,
Comics, and Scary Stories!
Sign up here!
YAAAS!

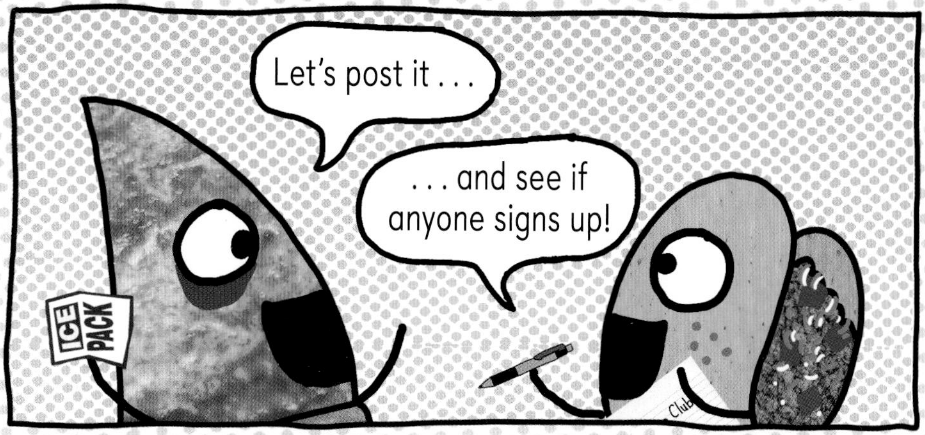
Let's post it . . .
. . . and see if anyone signs up!
ICE PACK
Club

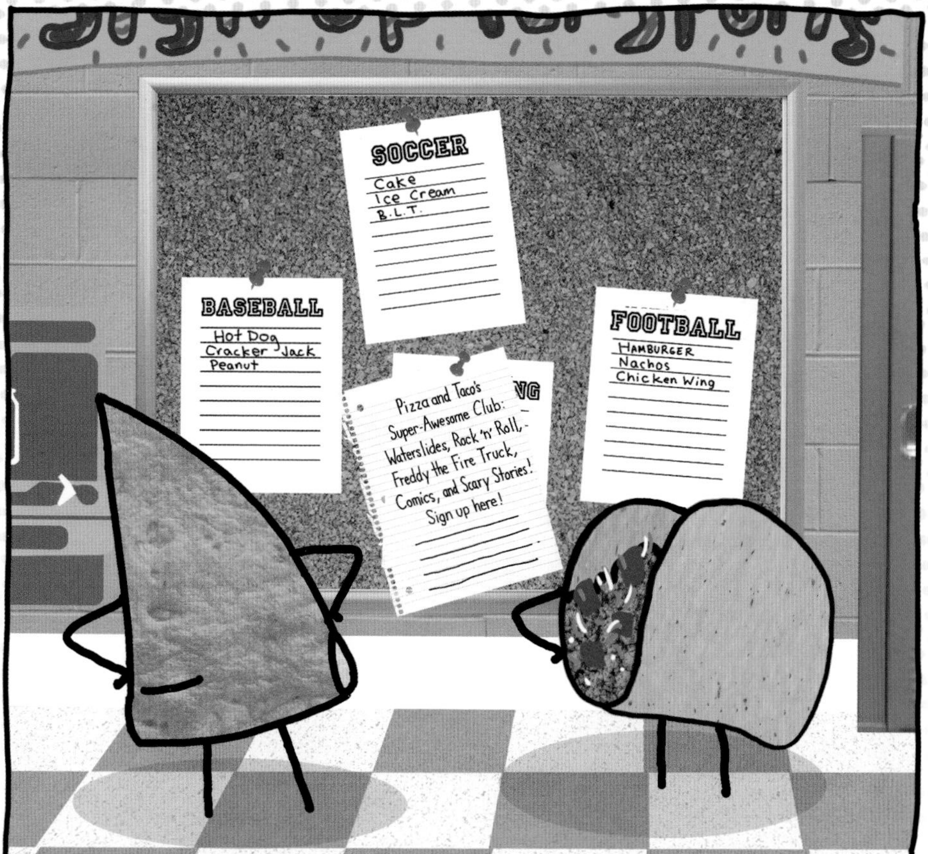
SOCCER
Cake
Ice Cream
B.L.T.
BASEBALL
Hot Dog
Cracker Jack
Peanut
FOOTBALL
HAMBURGER
Nachos
Chicken Wing
Pizza and Taco's Super-Awesome Club: Waterslides, Rock 'n' Roll, Freddy the Fire Truck, Comics, and Scary Stories! Sign up here!

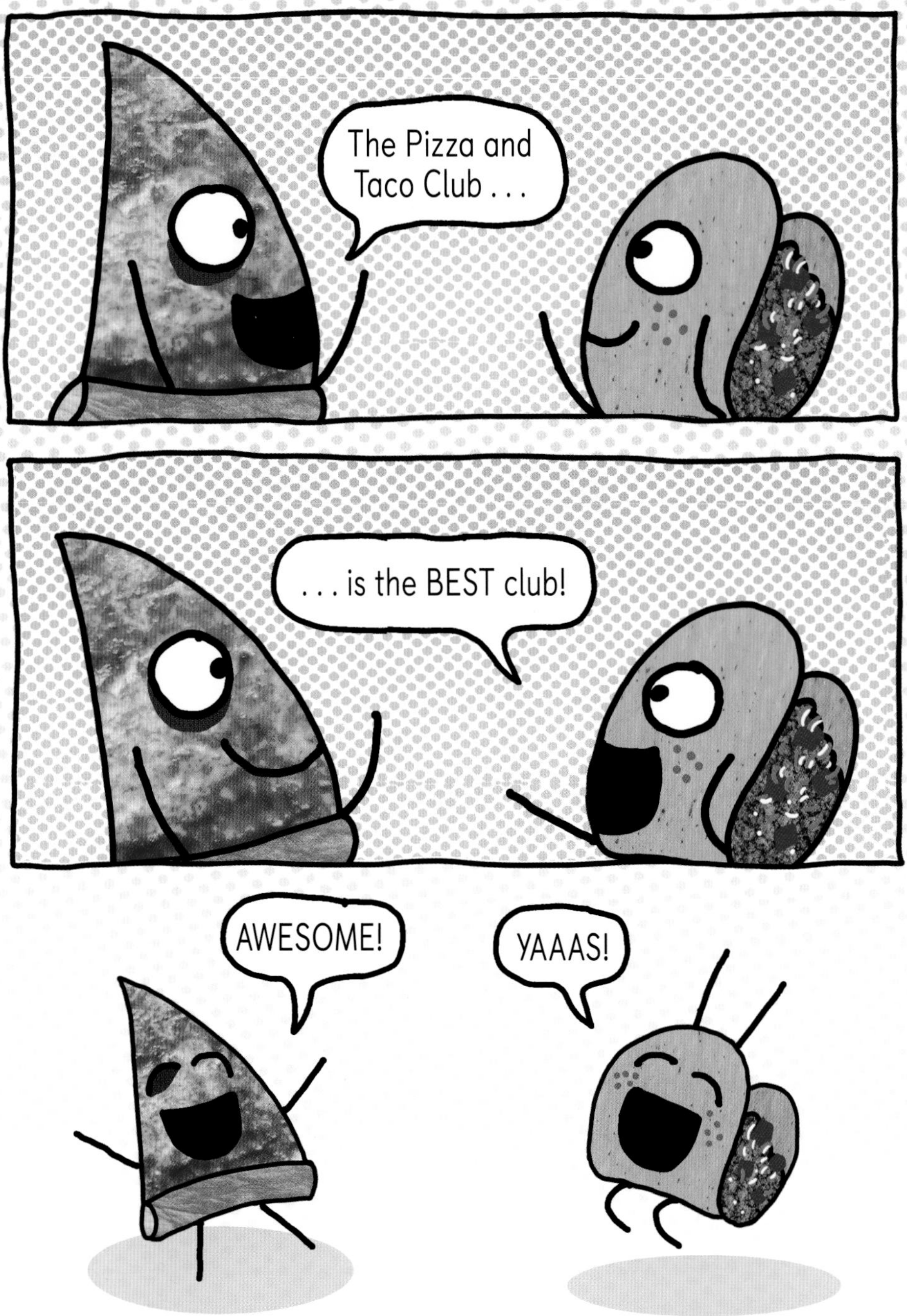
The Pizza and Taco Club . . .
. . . is the BEST club!
AWESOME!
YAAAS!

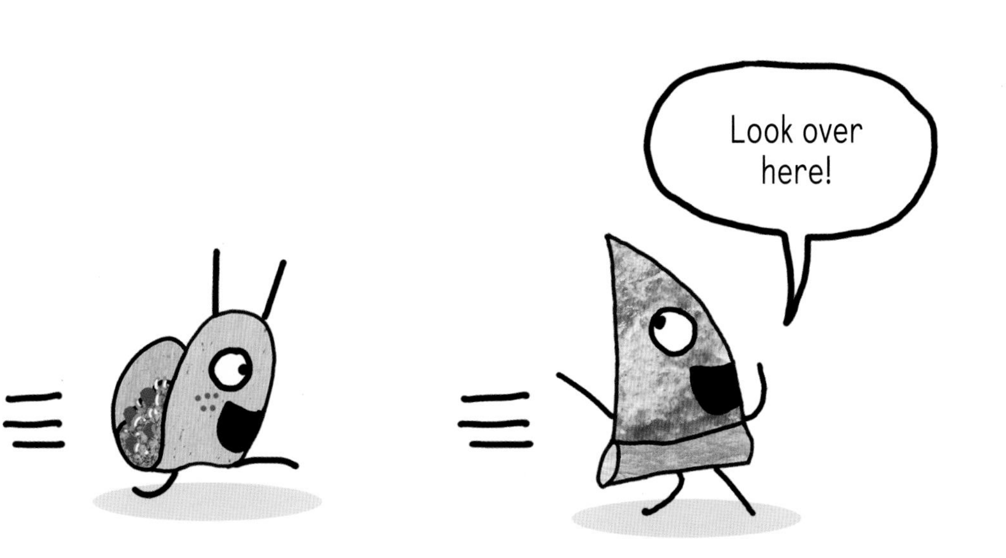
Look over here!

IT'S BEGINNING TO LOOK A LOT LIKE . . .

SNEAK PEEK!

CHRISTMAS!

PIZZA AND TACO HAVE PRETTY LONG WISH LISTS.

WILL SANTA SLAW BRING THEM EVERYTHING THEY WANT?

PRESENTS!

READ

PIZZA AND TACO: BEST CHRISTMAS EVER!

AND FIND OUT!

Coming in September 2024!

YAAAS!

AWESOME COMICS!
AWESOME KIDS!

SCAREDY'S NUTTY ADVENTURES

Scaredy Squirrel
In a Nutshell

MELANIE WATT

Kaeti Vandorn

MONSTER
Friends

Marshmallow
MART-ANS

Show and Smell

by Deanna Kent
illustrated by Neil Hooson

GNOME
and
Rat

Lauren Stohler

"I'm nutty for these sweet and silly squirrels."

ONE
SMART
COOKIE

Mika Song

Tig and Lily
Tiger Trouble

I'M A TIGER

Dan Thompson

GRUMPY MONKEY

WHO THREW
THAT?

By Suzanne Lang
Illustrated by Max Lang

PIZZA
and
TACO

WHO'S THE BEST?

STEPHEN SHASKAN

MARY POPE OSBORNE'S

MAGIC
TREE HOUSE
THE GRAPHIC NOVEL

DINOSAURS BEFORE DARK

adapted by JENNY LAIRD
illustrated by KELLY & NICHOLE MATTHEWS

Introduce your youngest reader to comics with

RH GRAPHIC

Learn more at RHCBooks.com

Background art (top to bottom); © 2023 by Mika Song; © 2023 by Melanie Watt; © 2023 by Stephen Shaskan

1446H

RHCB

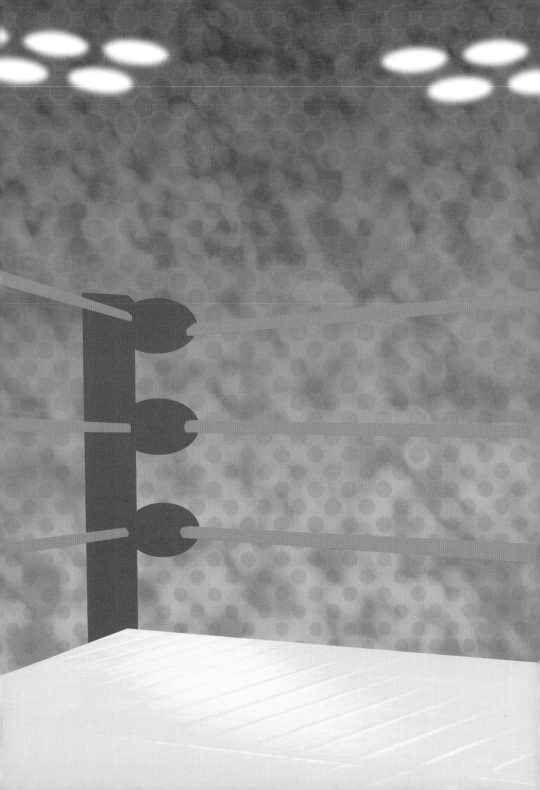